Clubbe Horace

Six satires

In a style between free imitation and literal version

Clubbe Horace

Six satires
In a style between free imitation and literal version

ISBN/EAN: 9783337283308

Printed in Europe, USA, Canada, Australia, Japan

Cover: Foto ©Andreas Hilbeck / pixelio.de

More available books at **www.hansebooks.com**

SIX
SATIRES of HORACE,

IN A STYLE BETWEEN

FREE IMITATION AND LITERAL VERSION.

•••••••••••••••◄◄✖✖►►•••••••••••

BY WILLIAM CLUBBE, LL. B.

VICAR OF BRANDESTON, SUFFOLK.

•••••••••••◄◄✖✖►►••••••••••

NEC VERBUM VERBO CURABIS REDDERE FIDUS
INTERPRES.———————————— *Hor.*

Printed and Sold by George Jermyn.
SOLD ALSO BY F. AND C. RIVINGTON, ST. PAUL'S CHURCH-YARD, AND
T. PAINE, MEWSE-GATE, LONDON.

M DCC XCV.

PREFACE.

MY motives for attempting to translate the Satires of *Horace* upon the plan now offered to the Public, were simply these.---Notwithstanding the difference in the Idiom of the languages, Dean *Swift* and Mr. *Pope* have clearly shewn that the spirit of this Author may in a great measure be preserved in our own. Their performances are indeed above all praise, and preclude competition : but in general they seem to me to have imitated (and that loosely) such parts of him only as suited the purpose of their own immediate Satire; and to have followed rather the train of thought than the exact sense of the Author.

Mr. *Francis*, on the contrary, is literal in the extreme; and does not allow himself (what I conceive every Translator is entitled to) the Liberty of using the Idioms of his own language, or changing an ancient custom for a modern one, however similar : indeed in the few instances that he does this, he seems to think it almost necessary to apologize for it. In short with all his excellencies, which are great and many, he appears to have forgotten the rule of his Author which I have adopted for my Motto.   To this literal adherence to ancient names, manners, and ideas, we may attribute his deficiency in that ease and humour which so strongly characterize the original. A Translation between these two extremes is my design; how far I have, or may further succeed in it, must now be decided by better, and I must suppose, less partial judges than myself.

To the *Classical* Reader I do not presume to give information; indeed I must be very well satisfied, if, in his judgment, I am allowed not to have mistaken the sense of *Horace* myself.   To preserve entirely, what in this part of his writings appear to me his peculiar beauties, a Satire severe without ill-humour, and a language familiar without vulgarity, I am sensible (to speak for myself at least) is not to be done. If I have put his admirable morality and sense into a form somewhat more intelligible to the *General* Reader, a great part of my wishes in this Publication will be gratified.

I am aware that an objection will lie against the mixture of ancient and modern names and allusions; but I must again beg leave to remark, that I do not mean either strictly to translate, or paraphrase; and have therefore stuck to my Author, or assumed a latitude in going from his literal sense, as suited my convenience. Where I have found any parallelism in *modern* manners and customs, I have introduced them; and where it has appeared necessary to the sense and intention of the Author, I have followed the Ideas of the original. In those Satires which consist wholly, or in part, of dialogue, I have left the names of the Speakers as I found them: for as no part of the sense or beauty of the Poem depended upon them, I did not see why I might not use the names of *Davus* and *Horace*, as well as any other that could have been substituted; indeed in the fifth Sat. of Lib. II. this was necessary; as it would have been impossible to have changed the persons of *Tiresias* and *Ulysses*, without losing a principal beauty in it; and for a similar reason, I have allowed myself fewer liberties of modernizing in this than in any other: in the last of the same Book, I have kept the original Dramatis Personæ for the opposite reason; because the persons of the Actors were indifferent to the Subject. Had I introduced modern ones, I must either have given them *fictitious* names, which I own, I had not ingenuity enough to invent; or real ones, which might have carried with them a personality which I wish as much as possible to avoid.

With respect to the intermixture of manners and allusions, where I have indulged myself in modernizing, I hope there will be found a sufficient similarity to warrant the liberty; though in other places I did not think myself entitled to lose sight of my Author's meaning, in running after a familiar idea.

Whether my plan be justifiable, or whether I have said enough to justify it, I know not; what I have offered is only meant (as the Lawyers say) in arrest of Judgment: let it only be remembered that I make no pretence to Depth of Erudition,---I am no Critic, nor a Reader of Critics.---Situated in a remote Village, I have had little access to Books, and as little to the Learned. My only wish has been to give my Version an air somewhat easier than that of a *literal* Translation; any errors therefore into which I may have fallen, the good natured Reader will excuse; and if any one is inclined to try me by a severer standard, let him recollect that I disclaim all Scholaftic importance, and have not its vanity to mortify.

BRANDESTON, JULY, 1795.

This * Asterism refers to a Note at the end.

List of Subscribers.

ABBOT, William, Esq. *New Inn, London*
Abel, Mr. *Weybread*
Acton, Nathaniel Lee, Esq. *Livermere*
Adams, Rev. S. *Ubbeston*
Adams, Mr. *London*
Allan, A. P. Esq. *Millgreen House, Essex*
Allan, Mrs. *Ditto*
Allen, Rev. Loder, *Easton*
Allen, —— Merchant, *Yarmouth*
Alderson, Robert, Esq.
Alderson, Edward Hall, Esq.
Amyas, Rev. —— *Henstead*
Anderson, F. Esq. *Customs*
Anderson, Robert, Surgeon, *Sudbury*
Andrew, D. M. Esq. *Customs*
Andrews, Robert, Esq. *Bulmer, Essex*
Andrews, Rev. Charles, *Henny, Ditto*
Anonymous, by Mr. Downing, *E. Soham*
Anonymous, by Ditto
Anonymous, *Easton*
Anonymous, *Mendham*
Anonymous, *Parham*
Anonymous
Antrobus, Philip, Esq. *London*, 2 copies

Antrobus, Rev. William, *London*
Applewhaite, Mr. Henry
Arcedeckne, Chaloner, Esq.
Ashford, Mr. Robert, *Earl Soham*
Athorpe, —— Esq. *St. John's, Cambridge*
Atkinson, Rev. W. *Ware, Herts.*
Avarne, Rev. Isaac, *Halesworth*
Ayton, William, Esq. *London*, 2 copies
Ayton, John, jun. Esq. *Ditto*, 4 copies
Ayton, Mrs. *Ditto*, 4 copies
Ayton, Miss Elizabeth Ann, *Ditto*, 4 copies
Ayton, John, Esq. *Earl Soham Lodge*, 2 c.
Ayton, Miss, *Ditto*, 2 copies
Ayton, Miss Jane, *Ditto*

Brome, Right Hon. Lord, 2 copies
Beaumont, Lady Dowager, *Essex*
Beaumont, Sir George, Bart. M.P. 4 copies
Bunbury, Sir Thos. Chas. Bart. M.P. 2 c.
Blois, Sir John, Bart. 4 copies
Bacon, Rev. Nicholas, M. A. *Coddenham*
Bacon, John, Esq.
Baldry, Mrs. *Earl Soham*
Barber, Mr.

Barne, Rev. Thomas, *Satterly*
Barnes, John, Esq. *London*, 2 copies
Barnwell, Rev. Fred. Henry, *Lawshall*
Barthorp, Mr. *Easton*
Bartlett, A. Surgeon, *Ipswich*
Barwis, Thomas, Esq. *London*, 2 copies
Bastard, —— Esq. *St. John's, Cambridge*
Bateman, Mr. Henry, *London*
Battye, John, Esq. *London*, 2 copies
Baynes, Rev. William, *Rickengale*, 2 copies
Beales, Mr. *Caius College, Cambridge*
Bedingfield, Mrs. *Ipswich*, 2 copies
Bedingfield, Rev Bacon, *Ditchingham*
Bedingfield,—— Esq. *St. John's, Cambridge*
Bellman, Rev. Rayner, *Wetheringsett*
Bellman, Rayner, Surgeon, *Earl Soham*
Berners, Charles, Esq. *Woolverston-hall*
Berners, Charles, jun. Esq. *Ditto*
Berners, Rev. Henry Denny, *Holbrook*
Betts, Rev. George, *Wortham*
Bevan, David, Esq. *London*
Bevan, Mr. T. S. *Barton, Norfolk*
Bevan, Sylvanus, Esq. *Riddlesworth, Ditto*
Bevan, David, Esq. *Ditto*
Bevan, Mr. Henry, *Ditto*
Bewick, Rev. T. *Harleston*
Bigsby, Thomas, M. D. *Ipswich*
Binns, John, Esq. *London*, 2 copies
Black, Mr. William, *Epping, Essex*
Black, Mr. John, *Ditto*
Black, Mr. Richard, *Jesus Coll. Cambridge*
Blake, Mr. Andrew, *Hoo*
Blakeney, —— Esq. *St. John's, Cambridge*
Blowers, Isaac, Esq. *Beccles*

Blowers, Rev. William, *Lavenham*
Bobbitt, Mr. John, *Toxford*
Bohun, L. B. Esq. *Beccles*
Bolton, Rev. William, *Hollesley*
Bond, Rev. Mr.
Bond, Rev. John
Boscawen, —— Esq. *London*
Bowen, Rev. Thomas, M. A. *Fulham Park*
Bowen, Rev. —— *Pulham*
Bower, Robert, Esq. *Welham, Yorkshire*
Bower, Mrs. *Ditto*
Bowles, Tobias, Gent. *London*
Bowles, John, Gent. *Sudbury*
Bowness, Rev. Francis, *Lowestoft*
Boyce, Rev. Thomas, *Waldingfield*
Bradbury, Rev. William, *Saling, Essex*
Bradbury, Wentworth, Esq. *Dunmow*
Bradbury, Rev. Thos. *Bradwell, Bucks.*
Bradley, Rev. William, *Aldborough*
Bradney, John, Esq. *Clapham*
Bramston, T. Berney, Esq. M. P. *Essex*
Brand, Wm. Beale, Esq. *Polstead Hall,*
Brand, John, Esq. *Hemingston*
Brandling, —— Esq. *St. John's, Cambridge*
Brassey, Nathaniel, Esq. *London*, 2 copies
Breun, Mr. Samuel, jun. *Yarmouth*
Bridge, Thomas, Esq. *Dunmow*, 2 copies
Brock, Rev. John, *Great Easton, Essex*
Broke, Philip Bowes, Esq. *Nacton*, 4 copies
Brooke, Rev. Zach. *St. John's, Cambridge*
Brooke, J. Gent. *Jesus College, Ditto*
Brooke, Francis, Esq. *Woodbridge*
Brooke, Rev. Charles, *Ditto*
Brown, Mr. *Trinity College, Cambridge*

Brown, Rev. Charles, *Blo-Norton*
Brown, Rev. William, *Saxmundham*
Browne, Rev. William, *Framlingham*
Buck, Rev. James, *Lavenham*
Bucke, Nathaniel, Surgeon, *Ipswich*
Buckle, Rev. Charles, *Worlingworth*
Buckle, Rev. William, *Wrentham*
Budworth, Rev. Richard, *High-Laver*, 2 c.
Bullock, John, Esq. M. P. *Essex*, 2 copies
Burrard, Peter, Esq. *Customs*
Burrough, F. Esq.
Burrough, Francis, Esq. *Sudbury*
Burrough, Rev. Samuel, *Heveningham*
Butterfield, Rev. James, *Canfield, Essex*
Butts, Rev. William, *Glemsford*

Chedworth, Right Hon. Lord, 2 copies
Cheere, Rev. Sir William, Bart.
Caldecot, Thomas, Esq. *Temple, London*
Caldwall, Mr. —— *Jesus College, Camb.*
Cancellor, John, Esq. *London*, 2 copies
Capper, Rev. Francis, *Earl Soham*, 6 copies
Capper, Rev. George, *Blakenham*, 4 copies
Carlyon, Rev. Tho. *Pemb. Coll. Cambridge*
Carpenter, William, Esq. 2 copies
Carpenter, Mrs.
Carthew, John, Gent. *Woodbridge*
Carthew, Rev. Morden, *Frittenham, Norf.*
Carter, John, Gent. *Ipswich*, 4 copies
Carter, Mrs. Elizabeth, *Deal*
Carter, Thomas, Gent. *Stonham*
Carter, Rev. Jonathan, *Flempton*
Catling, Mr. *Metfield*
Cazenove, James, Esq. *London*, 2 copies

Cazenove, Mrs. *London*, 2 copies
Cazenove, Henry, Esq. *Ditto*, 2 copies
Chamberlayne, Stanes, Esq.
Chandler, Mr. Thomas, *Felixstow*
Chevallier, Rev. Temple, *Aspal*
Chevallier, Rev. Temple, jun. *Badingham*
Chevallier, Rev. Clement, *Pemb.Coll.Camb.*
Clachar, Meggy, and Chalk, *Chelmsford*
Clarance, ——Surgeon, *Thaxted, Essex*
Clarke, William, Esq. *London*, 2 copies
Clarke, Rev. John, *Woodbridge*
Clarke, J. Esq. *Customs*
Claydon Book Club
Clayton, John, Esq.
Clerke, John, Surgeon, *Sudbury*
Close, Rev. H. Jackson, *Hitcham*, 4 copies
Clubbe, John, Surgeon, *Ipswich*
Clubbe, James, Gent. *Hoxne*, 4 copies
Clubbe, Charles, Attorney, *Dunmow*
Clubbe, Nathaniel, ditto, *Framlingham*
Clubbe, Thomas, ditto, *Sudbury*
Cobbold, Mrs. John, *Ipswich*, 2 copies
Coddenham Book Society
Coe, Mr. J. *Ipswich*
Coggan, James, Esq. *East India House*
Cole, Rev. William, *Yoxford*
Coleman, Mr. C. *Brockdish, Norfolk*
Collett, Rev. Anthony, *Cratfield*
Connor, Rev. John, *Orford*
Cooke, Rev. William, *Preston*
Cooper, Rev. Samuel, D. D. *Yarmouth*
Cooper, Rev. Lovick, *Ditto*
Cope, Thomas, Esq. *London*, 4 copies
Cornwell, Emerson, Esq. *Ipswich*

Cotton, Miss, *Claydon*
Cox, Rayner, Gent. *Hadleigh*
Coxe, Peter, Esq. 2 copies
Coyte, Wm. Beeston, M.D. *Ipswich*
Coyte, Rev. James, *Ditto*
Crabbe, Rev. George, *Parham*
Crabbe, Mrs. *Ditto*
Crickitt, C. A jun. Esq.
Crowe, Rev. Henry, *Burnham, Norfolk*
Crowe, Mr. Ph. *Swaffham, Ditto*
Crowfoot, John, Gent. *Kessingland*
Crowfoot, William, Surgeon, *Beccles*
Crowfoot, Wm. Henchman, *Ditto*
Cutting, Mr. Samuel, *Debenham*

Dysart, Rt. Hon. Earl of
Dysart, Rt. Hon. Countess of
Dalton, Mr. *Caius College Cambridge*
Dalton, —— Gent. *Bury,*
Dalton, Miss, *Ipswich*
Dalton, Mr. R. P.
Darby, Rev. Henry, *Groton*
Davie, Mr. John, *Sidney College, Cambridge*
Davie, John, Gent. *Debenham*
Davie, Mrs. *Ditto*
Davie, Mr. Jonathan, *Ditto*
Davie, Mr. Jonathan, jun. *Ditto*
Davie, Mr. Samuel, *Hadleigh*
Davie, Mar. Launcelot, *Gram. Sch. Ipswich*
Davy, Eleazar, Esq. *Yoxford*, 4 copies
Davy, David Elisha, Esq. Receiver General
Davy, Rev. Charles, *Combs*
Dawes, William, Esq. *London*, 2 copies
Dawson, Rev. Henry, 2 copies

Dawson, S. T. Esq. *St. John's, Cambridge*
Dent, Digby, Esq. *Ipswich*
De St. Luc, Charles, Esq. 2 copies
Devins, Richard, Esq. *Customs*
Dickinson, Henry, Esq. *East India House*
Dinsdale, Rob. M. D. *Bishop's-Stortford*
Dominicus, G. Esq. *East India House,* 4 c.
Doughty, George, Esq. *Theberton*
Dove, Rev. John, *Ipswich*
Downing, Mr. *Earl Soham*
Drake, William, Esq. M. P. *London*
Drake, William, jun. Esq. M. P. *Ditto*
Drake, Rev. J. LL. D. *Ditto*
Drake, Nathan, M. D. *Hadleigh*
Dreyer, Mrs. *Harleston*
Dreyer, Rev. R. *Yarmouth*
Drury, Richard Vere, Esq. *East Bergholt*
Duboulay, Mrs. *London,* 2 copies

Eade, Rev. Peter, *Weybread*
Edgar, Mileson, Esq. *Ipswich*
Edge, Rev. John, *Ditto*
Edwards, William, Esq. *London,* 2 copies
Edwards, Rev. —— *Yarmouth*
Edwards, Thomas, Surgeon, *Melford*
Ellicott, Rev. T. *Tavywell, Northamptonshire*
Ellis, Thos. Flower, Esq. *London,* 2 copies
Esdaile, James, Esq. *London,* 2 copies
Esdaile, Mrs. *Ditto,* 2 copies
Esdaile, Miss, *Ditto,* 2 copies
Esdaile, Thomas, Esq. *Ditto,* 2 copies
Etheredge, Rev. Robert, *Starston*
Etheredge, Mr. T. *Fressingfield*
Evans, Samuel, Esq. *Ongar, Essex*

Earl Soham Book Society
Everard, Miss, *Harleston*
Everitt, William, Gent. *Walton*
Eyles, Mr. W. A. *East India House*

Farmer, Rev. Rich. D.D. *Eman.Coll.Camb.*
Fawcett, Rev. James, *St. John's, Cambridge*
Fenton, Thomas, Esq. *Pemb. Coll. Camb.*
Field, William, Esq. *Canonbury Place*
Field, William, jun. Esq. *Chatham Place*
Ficklin, Rev. Robert, *Lamas, Norfolk*
Fletcher, Rev. —— *Beckenham, Kent*
Ford, John, Esq. *Sproughton*
Forester, Rev. Henry, *Leigh, Kent*
Forster, Rev. Peter, *Hedingham, Norfolk*
Forster, Mr. P. *Ipswich*
Forby, Rev. Robert, *Barton, Norfolk*
Fowke, William, Esq. *Market-Weston*
Frampton, —— Esq. *St. John's, Cambridge*
Frank, Rev. Richard, D.D. *Alderton*, 4 c.
French, James, Surgeon, *Harleston*
French, Thomas, Gent. *Eye*
Frost, Mr. Thomas, *Brent-Eleigh*
Fulcher, Mr. Thomas, *Ipswich*
Fuller, Mr. Nathaniel, *Hoo-Hall*
Fuller, Mr. James, *Brandeston*

Gooch, Sir Thomas, Bart. *Benacre*
Gallant, Mr. Henry, *Ipswich*
Galley, —— Esq. *London*, 2 copies
Garret, Mr. John, *Kettleburgh*
Gee, Rev. William, *Ipswich*, 4 copies
Gepp, Mr. Thomas Frost, *Chelmsford*
Gepp, Mr. G. A. Surgeon, *Ditto*

Gibbs, Rev. L. *Brockdish*
Gibson, Rev. Thomas, *Ipswich*
Gibson, John, Esq. *Ditto*
Gillbee, William, Esq. *London*, 2 copies
Girdlestone, R. M.D. *Yarmouth*
Girdlestone, Mrs. *Ditto*
Girdlestone, Rev. W. *Kelling, Norfolk*
Glover, Rev. Edward, *Norwich*
Goate, E. Esq. *Col. East Suffolk Militia*
Golding, George, Esq. *Thorington*, 4 copies
Golightly, William, Esq. *London*, 2 copies
Goodenough, Rev. Samuel, D. D. *Ealing*
Goodwin, William, Gent. *Earl Soham*
Goodwin, Rev. James, *Cambridge*
Goodwin, Rev. —— *Christ's Coll. Camb.*
Gostling, Mr. *Ipswich*
Graves, Rev. Morgan, *Redgrave*
Graves, Rev. George Golding, *Kelsale*
Gray, Richard, Esq. *Somerset Place*
Gray, Robert, Esq. *London*
Green, Miss, *Bury*
Green, Mr. *Harleston*
Green, Mr. *Debenham*
Gretton, Mr. Surgeon, *Colchester*
Griggs, G. Esq. *Messing*
Grimwood, Rev. T. Lech. D.D. *Dedham*
Groom, Robinson, Gent. *Aldborough*
Gunning, Rev. Joseph, *Sutton*
Gurdon, Theophilus, Esq. *Letton, Norf.*

Hewet, Rev. Sir Thomas, Bart. *Nacton*
Henniker, Sir John, Bart.
Harland, Lady, *Ipswich*
Harland, Sir Robert, Bart. *Wherstead Lodge*

d

Hales, —— Esq. *St. John's, Cambridge*
Halifax, Mr. 2 copies
Hammond, William, Gent. *Ipswich*
Hammond, John, Merchant, *Woodbridge*
Hammond, P. H. Esq. *Essex*
Harris —— Esq. *St. John's, Cambridge*
Harrington, J. Gastrel, *Hartest*
Harrington, Joseph, Gent. *Clare*, 4 copies
Harris, Mr. Robert, *Ipswich*
Harrison, P. Surgeon, *Diss*
Hase, Edward, Gent. *Ipswich*
Harsant, Martin, Gent. *Earl Soham*
Harsant, Thomas, Surgeon, *Wickham M.*
Harsant, John, Gent. *Brandeston*
Harvey, Rev. Richard, *Ramsgate, Kent*
Harvey, Rev. R. jun. *Isle of Thanet, Ditto*
Haverfield, John, Esq. *Kew Green*
Haverfield, Mrs. *Ditto*
Haynes, Rev. C. M. *Witnesham*
Henchman, Wm. Surgeon, *E. Soham*, 4 c.
Henchman, Mrs. *Ditto*, 4 copies
Henchman, Mar. Wm. Gram. Sch. *Ipswich*
Henley, Rev. Samuel, *Rendlesham*
Herring, William, Esq. *Norwich*
Hewitt, Rev. —— *Queen's Coll. Cambridge*
Hill, Rev. Henry, *Buxhall*
Hingeston, Rev. Samuel, *Boyton*
Hippoff, Charles, Esq. *London*, 2 copies
Hobden, Rev. Edward, *Barsham*
Holder, J. W. B M. *Bungay*
Holland, John, Esq. *East India House*
Holmes, Rev. Gervas, *Gawdy-Hall Norf.*
Holmes, Thomas, Esq. *South Town*
Holt, Thomas, Esq. *Redgrave*

Houblon, J. Esq *Hallingbury Place, Essex*
Howard, Rev. —— *Houghton, Bucks.*
Howlett, Rev. John, *Dunmow*
Hughes, Rev. T. *Prebend of Westminster*, 4 c.
Hunt, Mr J. *Chillesford*

Jackson, John, Esq.
Jenner, —— Esq. *St. John's, Cambridge*
Jennion, Joseph, Esq. *East India House*
Jenny, Edmund, Esq. *Bungay*
Jermyn, Peter, Gent *Halesworth*
Jermyn, George, *Ipswich*
Jephson, Rev. Graham, *Fulham*
Johnson, Robert, Esq. *London*, 2 copies
Johnson, Capt. Benjamin, *Bailham*
Johnson, Rev. Maurice, D.D. *Spalding*
Jones, Griffith, Esq. *London*, 2 copies
Jones, —— Gent. *Gray's Inn*, 2 copies
Jones, Rev. R. *St. John's, Cambridge*
Jones, Rev. William, F. R. S. *Nayland*
Jordan, Joseph, Esq. *East India House*
Ipswich Book Club
Iselin, J. L. Esq. *Norwich*
Ives, Rev. J. Clement, *Bungay*

Kedington, Rev. Roger, *Rougham*
Keer, Davie, Surgeon, *Framlingham*
Kellett, Henry, Esq. *London*
Kempthorne, Mr. *St. John's, Cambridge*
Kent, Mr. Thomas, *Ipswich*
Kerrich, John, jun. Esq. *Harleston*
Kerrich, Mr. Edward, *Ditto*
Kerrison, Matthias, Esq.
Keymer, Wm. Printer, *Colchester*

Kilderbee, Samuel, Gent. *Ipswich*
Kilderbee, Rev Samuel, *Campsey Ash*, 4 c.
King, Rev. John, *Ipswich*
King, Rev. J. W. *Braughing, Herts.*
King, Rev. Shaw, *Thorp, Essex*
Kirby, John, Gent. *Ipswich*
Kirby, Rev. William, *Barham*, 2 copies
Kirby, Mrs. *Ditto*
Kirkland, William, M.D. *Chelmsford*

Lambert, John, Esq. *London*, 2 copies
Lambert, Rev. James, *Fell.Trin Coll.Camb.*
Langdale, Marmaduke, Esq. *London*, 2 c.
Larkins, Mr. John, *Puckeridge, Herts.*
Lathbury, Rev. Peter, *Woodbridge*
Law, Rev. J. D D *Archdeacon of Rochester*
Law, Rev. George, *Kelshall, Herts.*
Law, Mrs *Pulham*
Lawton, Robert, Esq. *Ipswich*
Lawton, Rev. Henry, *Ashbocking*
Layton, Rev. William, *Ipswich*
Leake, Rev. John, *Willisham*
Leake, J. B. Gent. *Hadleigh*
Leatherdale, Mr. *Harleston*
Leatherdale, Mr. Richard, *Hadleigh*
Leathes, Rev. J *Fell. Jesus Coll. Camb.*
Lee, George, Esq. 4 copies
Lee, Richard, A. Esq. 2 copies
Lee, Richard, Esq. 2 copies
Lee, Robert, Esq. 2 copies
Leedes, John, Gent. *Coddenham*
Leedes, William, Gent. *Hemingston*
Leggate, Rev. —— *Isle of Wight*
Leggatt, Rev. F.

Lewis, Rev. John, *Bungay*
Lewis, Miss, *Helmingham*
Lloyd, Mr. T. D *East India House*
Lloyd, Mr. T. G. *Ditto*
Lock, Peter, Esq. *Customs*
Lockwood, Rev J.
Loder, Mr. Robert, *Woodbridge*
Lofft, Capel, Esq. *Troston Hall*
Long, Charles, Esq *Saxmundham*
Longe, Rev. John, M. A. *Henley*
Lowndes, William, Esq. *Winslow, Bucks.*
Lumkin, Rev. John, *Grundisburgh*, 2 copies
Lynch, William, Esq. *Ipswich*
Lypeat, Rev. Jonathan

Maynard, Right Hon. Lord Viscount
Maber, Peter, Esq. *Foxhall*
Mackenzie, Colin, Esq. *London*, 2 copies
Maclean, L. M.D. *Sudbury*
Major, John Henniker, Esq. M.P.
Mann, Gibson, Gent. *Ipswich*
Mann, Rev. Thomas, *Coddenham*
Mann, Mr. *Syleham*
Manning, Alderman, Esq. *Peasenhall*
Mapletoft, Rev Edmund, *Ainsty, Herts.*
Marlow, Rev.Mich D.D. *St. John's, Oxf. 2 c.*
Marriott, John, Esq. *Finchingfield, Essex*
Marriott, Richard, Esq. *Ditto*
Marriott, Rev. Robert, *Needham*
Marsham, Thomas, Esq. *London*
May, Rev. —— *London*, 2 copies
Maynard, Thomas, Esq. *Hoxne*
Maynard, Rev. Henry, *Thaxted, Essex*
Meadows, Mr. Philip, *C. C. C. Cambridge*

Merest, Rev. James, *Wortham*

Methold, Rev. Thomas, *Stonham*, 4 copies

Middleton, William, Esq *Crowfield*, 2 c.

Middleton, Henry, Esq. *Ditto*, 2 copies

Milles, Rich. Esq. *N. Elmham, Norf.* 2 c.

Mills, —— Surgeon, *Pulham*

Mills, Rev. Edward, *Bury*

Milner, John, Esq. *Customs*

Moore, Mrs *Christ Church*

Moore, Miss, *Claydon*

Moor, Lieut. Edward, *Woodbridge*

Moreton, Rev. Robert J. *Canfield, Essex*

Morphew, John, Gent. *Norwich*

Morphew, Mr. J. *Cross, King's Coll. Camb.*

Morris, —— Esq. *St. John's, Cambridge*

Moxon, Mr. *Weybread*

Mudd, John, Gent. *Lavenham*

Mundy, Mr. Frederick, *Barton, Norfolk*

Mundy, Mr. Henry, *Ditto*

Mure, James, Esq.

Naffau, George, Esq. *Trimly*, 20 copies

Nealson, James, Esq. *London*, 2 copies

Newman, Rev. Thomas, *Little Bromley*

Newson, James, Gent. *Bruisyard*

Norcross, Rev. John, *Fell. Pemb. Coll. Camb.*

North, Dudley, Esq. M.P. *Glemham*

Notcutt, Thomas Foster, Gent. *Ipswich*

Nottidge, Rev. John, *East Hanningfield*

Nottidge, Josias, jun. Esq. *Bocking*

Nottidge, J. Thos. Esq. *Trin. Coll. Camb.*

Orgil, Rev. —— *Worlingham*

Outram, —— Esq. *St. John's, Cambridge*

Paddon, Rev. George

Page, Mr. *Pulham*

Palmer, Rev. George Jones, *Ufford*, 2 c.

Parsons, George, Surgeon, *Hadleigh*

Parsons, Mrs. *Ditto*

Parsons, Miss Charlotte, *Ditto*

Parsons, G. C. Gent. *Dunmow*

Parsons, Rev. Philip, *Wye, Kent*

Parsons, Rev. John Weddel

Parsley, Mr. *Harleston*

Patteson, Mrs. *Norwich*

Patteson, Rev. Henry, *Weston*, 2 copies

Paxton, Rev. H. *Battisford*

Pearce, Thomas, Gent. *Combs*

Pearce, Thomas, Gent. *Carlton*, 2 copies

Pearl, John, Gent. *Hoxne*

Pearson, William, Gent. *Ipswich*

Pearson, Mr. Jasper, *Framlingham*

Pearson, Rev. E. *Fell. Sidney Coll. Camb.*

Pemberton, Rev. Edward, *Foxearth*

Penn, Rev. J. *Beccles*

Pern, Rev. Andrew, *Abington, Cambridges.*

Petit, Mr. *Queen's Coll. Cambridge*

Pettiward, Rev. D. *Coddenham*

Pettiward, Mar. George Douglas, *Putney*

Phillips, Charles, Esq. *Langford, Essex*, 2 c.

Phillips, Rev. Charles, *Ditto*

Philips, Mr.

Philpot, Mr. William, *Huntingfield*

Pickering, G. C. Esq. *Staffordshire*, 2 copies

Pickering, Miss, *Herts.* 2 copies

Pierson, Peter, Esq. *Inner Temple*, 4 copies

Pigot, John Coe, Esq. *Maldon, Essex*

Pillener, James, Esq. *London*, 2 copies

Pitcher, Mr. John, *Brandeston*
Plampin, John, Esq. *Shimpling*
Plampin, Rev. John, *Whatfield*
Plampin, Rev. George, *Melford*
Platt, John, Esq. *London*, 2 copies
Plestow, Rev. John Davis, *Ipswich*
Poole, Mr. *Harleston*
Powys, —— Esq. *St. John's, Cambridge*
Pretyman, Mr. H. N. *Brockdish*
Proby, Rev. N. Charles, *Stratford*
Purvis, Charles, Esq. *Darsham*
Purvis, Mrs. *Ipswich*
Purvis, —— Surgeon, *Beccles*
Pye, Rev. H. Anth. *Lapworth, Warwicks.*

Quilter, Mr. Samuel, *Felixstow*

Rochford, Right Hon. Earl of, 20 copies
Rich, Rev. Sir Charles, Bart. 2 copies
Rous, Sir John, Bart. M.P. 20 copies
Rowley, Sir William, Bart. *Tendring Hall*
Rowley, Lady, *Ditto*
Rabbett, Reginald, Esq. *Bramfield*
Rackham, Mr. Bookseller, *Bury*
Ray, Samuel, Gent. *Worlingworth*
Ray, William, Gent. *Tannington*
Ray, Rev. J Mead, *Sudbury*
Raymond, Rev. S. *Belchamp-hall, Essex*
Raynsford, Robert, Esq. *Essex*
Rede, Thomas, Esq. *Beccles*
Rede, Robert, Esq. *Ditto*
Reeve, Samuel, Esq. *Rear Admiral of White*
Reeve, Rev. Thomas, *Bungay*
Revett, Nicholas, Esq. *London*

Revett, John, Esq. *Brandeston Hall*, 12 c.
Revett, Mrs. 4 copies
Revett, J. C. Esq. *Pemb.Coll.Camb.* 4 copies
Revett, John, Surgeon, *Debenham*
Reynolds, Rev. Robert, *De-Boulge*
Rhodes, Mr. *Caius Coll. Cambridge*
Rhudde, Rev. Durand, D.D. *East-Bergholt*
Riley, Rev. R. *St. John's Coll. Cambridge*
Riley, Mr. William, *Bury*
Ripley, Rev. Richard
Ripper, Mr. Daniel, *Framsden*
Roberts, Thos. jun. Esq. *London*, 2 copies
Robinson, Rev. J.
Rodbard, John, M. D. *Ipswich*
Rodwell, Thomas, Esq. *London*, 2 copies
Rodwell, Mr. *St. John's, Cambridge*
Roope, Mr. G. *Pulham*
Roper, C. B. Esq. *Customs*
Round, George, Esq. *Colchester*
Routh, Rev. George, *Ipswich*
Rowley, Joshua, Esq. *Tendring Hall*
Ruggles, Thomas, Esq. *Clare*
Rush, George, Esq. *Benhall Lodge*, 2 c.
Rustat, Mrs. *Ipswich*

Smyth, Sir William, Bart.
Safford, Rev. —— *Beccles*
Salmon, Mr. Samuel, *Jesus Coll. Cambridge*
Salusbury, J. L. Esq. *Pemb. Coll.Camb.* 4 c.
Satterthwaite, Miles, Esq. *London*, 2 copies
Savage, Mr. *Ipswich*
Sayers, Francis, M. D. *Norwich*
Scott, Captain, *Loyal Essex Fencibles*
Scott, Mrs.

Schrieber, William, Esq *Wickham Market*
Selby, Miss, *Ipswich*
Sharpe, Rev. John, *Ipswich*
Sheppard, John, Esq. *Campsey-Ash*, 2 c.
Sheppard, Thomas, Esq. *Thornton Hall*
Sheppard, Mr. Revett, *Barham*
Sheriff, Rev. T.
Shield, Rev. T. *St. John's, Cambridge*
Short, Henry Hazard, Esq. *Boulge Hall*
Shreeve, Mr. William, *Yarmouth*
Silburn, Mr. Luke, *Ipswich*
Silke, Rev. Angel, *Stebbing, Essex*
Skellett, Henry, Esq. *London*
Slack, Rev. Matthew, *Sudbury*
Slapp, Mr. *Christ's College, Cambridge*
Smalles, Richard, Esq. *London*, 2 copies
Smallwood, Charles, Esq. *E. India House*
Smith, William, Esq. *London*, 2 copies
Smith, Rev. J. *St. John's, Cambridge*
Smith, Rev. —— *Bucks.*
Smith, Mr. Michael, *Academy, Writtle*
Smith, Rev. John Gee, *Chelsworth*
Smith, Mrs. *Denmow*
Smyth, Joseph Burch, Gent. *Sproughton*
Smythe, George, Esq. *Harleston*
Smythies, Rev. H.
Smythies, Rev. Yorick, *Colchester*
Smythies, H. Y. *Fell. Eman. Coll. Camb.*
Sumner, Rev. Humphrey, D. D. *Copdock*
Snodgrass, Gabriel, Esq. *Blackheath*
Spark, William, Surgeon, *Ipswich*
Sparke, John, Gent. *Walsham*
Sparrow, Robert, Esq. *Worlingham*, 4 c.
Sparrow, Rev. Bence, *Beccles*, 4 copies

Sperling, Henry, Esq. *Dynes Hall*, 2 copies
Spilsbury, J. Esq. *Customs*
Squire, Edmund, Gent, *Bury*, 2 copies
Stanford, John, Gent. *Framlingham*
Starkie, Nicholas, Esq. *Dickleburgh*, 2 copies
Steen, William, Esq. *London*, 2 copies
Steers, Charles, Esq. *London*, 2 copies
Stevens, Mr. *London*
Stevens, Mrs. *Ditto*
Stewart, Rev. Charles Edw. *Long Melford*
Stisted, Mrs. *Ipswich*
Stisted, Charles, Esq. *Ditto*
Stoe, Harry, Esq. *London*, 2 copies
Stone, Rev. George, *Hopton*
Strachey, Rev. John, LL.D. *Archd. Suff.* 4 c.
Stratford Book Club
Strutt, J. Holden, Esq. M. P. *Essex*
Suggate, Mr. George, jun. *Halesworth*
Sutton, Rev. Charles, *Norwich*, 2 copies
Sutton, Robert, Esq. *London*, 2 copies
Sutton, John, Esq. *Ditto*, 2 copies
Syer, Rev. Dyc, D. D. *Kedington*
Syer, Rev. Isaac Neville, *Waldingfield*
Symes, Rev. M. *Roothing*

Thorowgood, Lady, *Sampson's Hall, Suffolk*
Talbot, Rev. Wm. *Chancellor of Salisbury*, 4 c.
Taylor, Rev. William, *Swaffham*
Taylor, Rev. H. *Eccles*
Taylor, Rev. T. *Dedham*
Taylor, Samuel, Gent. *Gray's Inn*, 2 copies
Templeman, Peter, Esq. *London*, 2 copies
Terry, Christopher, Esq. *Ditto*, 2 copies
Theed, Thomas, Esq. *Edmonton, Middlesex*

Thelwall, Watkin, Esq. *Ottley*, 4 copies

Theobald, J. Meadows, Esq. *Claydon Hall*

Thompson, John, Esq.

Thwaites, T. G. W. Esq. *Customs*

Tillard, Rev. R. *St. John's, Cambridge*

Tindall, R. Gent. *Chelmsford*

Tindall, Mr. N. *Ditto*

Toosey, Mr. Joseph, *Ipswich*

Towgood, Matthew, Esq. *London*, 2 copies

Trant, Rev. Edmund, *Toft, Cambridgeshire*

Trimmer, Mrs. *Old Brentford*

Trimmer, Mr. Joshua, *Ditto*

Trimmer, Miss Julia, *Ditto*

Trimmer, Mr. William, *Ditto*

Trotman, Robert, Esq. *Ipswich*

Trotman, Mrs. R. *Ditto*

Trower, James, Esq.

Trusson, Thomas, Esq. *Kelsale*

Tunstall, Robert, Esq. *Kew Green*

Tunstall, Miss, *Ditto*

Tunstall, Miss F. *Ditto*

Turner, Mrs. *Ipswich*, 2 copies

Turner, Whichcote, Esq. *Ditto*, 2 copies

Turner, Rev. Joseph, D.D. *Dean of Norwich*

Turner, G. Esq. *St. John's, Cambridge*

Turner, Rev. G. *Kettleburgh*

Turner, Miss, *Harleston*

Turner, Charles, Gent. *Toxford*

Turner, Rev. R. *Yarmouth*

Tweed, Rev. Joseph, *Capel*

Tweed, John, Surgeon, *Bocking*

Twiss, Richard, Esq. *London*

Uthoff, Rev. Henry, *Huntingfield*

Uvedale, Rev. Ambrose, *Barking*

Uvedale, Rev. W. *Wenhaston*

Vaughan, Rev. Edward, *Fressingfield*

Venning, Mr. W. *London*

Verden, Rev. Henry, *Chislet, Kent*

Waddington, Rev. Richard, *Cavendish*

Wade, George, Esq. *London*, 2 copies

Wade, George, Gent. *Dunmow, Essex*

Wade, Mark, Gent. *Reydham*

Wade, Rev. William, *St John's, Cambridge*

Wade, John, *Emanuel Coll. Cambridge*

Wagstaffe, Mr. *Harleston*

Wakeman, Rev. H. *Bocking*

Wallis, David, Esq. *London*, 2 copies

Wallis, J. E. Esq. *Colchester*

Wallis, Rev. Bailey, *Ipswich*

Warburton, Rev. *Archdeacon, Harleston*

Warburton, Mrs. *ditto*

Warburton, Rev. Wm. P. *Lambeth*, 2 c.

Warren, Richard, M. D. *London*

Watson, Rev. George, D.D. *Hadleigh*

Watts, Robert, Esq. *London*, 2 copies

Wayth, Thomas, Gent. *Oakley*

Wayth, Mrs. *ditto*

Webb, Mr. *Pulham*

Westhorp, Mrs. *Foxford*

Western, Chas. Callis, Esq. M. P. *Essex*

Whishaw, Charles, Gent. *London*, 2 copies

Whishaw, Mrs. *Ditto*, 2 copies

Whishaw, John, Gent. *Gray's Inn*, 2 copies

Whishaw, Hugh, Gent. *London*, 2 copies

Whishaw, Mrs. *Chester*, 2 copies

Whishaw, Mrs. Sarah, *Ditto*, 2 copies

Whishaw, Mrs. Ann, *Chester*, 2 copies

Whishaw, Miss, 2 copies

Whitaker, Rev. Thomas, *Mendham*

Whitbread, Jacob, Esq. *Loudham-Hall*

White, J. Esq. *Major East Suffolk Militia*

White, R. G. Gent. *Halesworth*

White, Edward, Gent. *Kessingland*

Whitmore, Rev. G. *St. John's, Cambridge*

Wilgress, Rev. John, D. D.

Williams, Richard, Esq. *Customs*

Wiseman, Mr. B. *Diss*

Wix, Rev. S. *Christ's Coll. Cambridge*

Wolfe, John, Esq. *Walden, Essex*

Wolfe, Thomas, Esq. *Ditto*

Wood, Miss, *Bury*

Wood, Rev. J. *St. John's Cambridge*

Wood, George, Esq. *Pall Mall*, 4 copies

Wood, William, Esq. *London*, 2 copies

Wood, John, Esq. *Ditto*, 2 copies

Wood, Rev. Barker Finis, *Claydon*

Woodbridge Book Society

Woodcock, John, Gent. *Halesworth*

Woodward, —— Esq.

Worth, W. C. Esq. *Norwich*

Wright, Mr. *Academy, Gorleston*

Wyatt, Rev. William, *Framlingham*, 4 c.

Wyatt, John, *Jesus Coll. Cambridge*

Wyld, Mr.

Wynne, Rev. William, *Dennington*

Wynyeve, William, Esq. *Brettenham*

ADDITIONAL SUBSCRIBER.

Banks, Rev. John, *Master Grammar School, Boston*

HORATII

LIB. I. EPIST. XX. *Ad* LIBRUM SUUM.

Vertumnum Janumque, liber, ...

IMITATED.

Go thy conceited way---so proud to look
Through *Jermyn's* Window, a neat printed book;
Yes! to be public, scorn the private friend
Who sees, and wou'd thy many faults amend :
Go!---but, too late, I hear thee mournful cry,   5
" Ah, headstrong wish! ah, childish vanity!
" Better have rested where I was obscure,
" Than thus provoke the *Critical Reviewer!*

B

" Or once, perhaps, in careless haste be read,
" And then, cramm'd into pocket heels and head."   10

Full well, if passion blind me not, I see
How short thy date of popularity :
Pleasing at first, but in a corner thrown,
When thy best charm---thy novelty is gone.
How many copies, left, the seas must pass,   15
Sent with the last year's papers to *Madras !*
How many o'er the vast Atlantic rove,
With other Convicts bound for *Sydney Cove!*
Or, what I think far better on my troth,
Rest where they are---the bed and food of moth.   20

In either situation when I see
Thy pride thus hurt, the laugh will be with me ;
But let the Ass, if such the creature's will,
Tumble from top to bottom of the hill.
Perhaps some Master of a Country School,   25
Who scarce of Latin knows a single rule,

May think five shillings not quite thrown away
To steal from thee the Lesson of the day.

    Amongst the gaping croud, shou'd one desire
To know your Author, or his name enquire,   30
Say, in few words,---his Father was a Priest,
And of the reverend Order not the least:
A Bishop? no: a Canon? not so high:
A Country Parson on a Rectory:
A Country Parson,---but his Children's pride,   35
That in his virtues he was dignified.

    With income, for his notions much too small,
His Son makes out to live, and that is all:
Inclin'd to soar, he chance a dinner gives,
That only leads to question, how he lives: 40
Acquaintance rather large, but nothing higher,
Nor does he court it, than the Country Squire:
Unfit for deeper studies, pleas'd with rhyme,
And, from late illness, *grey* before his time:

Of middle stature, fond to bask away   45
In Sun and indolence the ſummer's day:
Prone to dispute, if chance he takes a cup,
But never known to keep resentment up.

Shou'd one, more curious, teaze you to be told
Exactly to a year or month how old,---   50
Fifteen when GEORGE the *Third* his reign begun,
And now just entering upon *Fifty one*.

SELECT

SATIRES

OF

HORACE.

LIBER PRIMUS.

SAT. I. Ad MÆCENATEM.

QUI fit, Mæcenas, ut nemo, quam sibi sortem,
Seu ratio dederit, seu fors objecerit, illâ
Contentus vivat; laudet diversa sequentes!

O fortunati Mercatores! gravis armis
Miles ait, multo jam fractus membra labore.
Contra Mercator, navim jactantibus Austris,
Militia est potior: Quid enim? concurritur: horæ
Momento cita mors venit, aut victoria læta.

FIRST BOOK.

SAT. I. To MÆCENAS.

STRANGE, that the various extended field
Of human search, should no contentment yield!
As strange, that men a preference shou'd give
To any kind of Life than that they live!

Ask of yon *Soldier*, why he quits his arms?   5
Tir'd, he will say, of War and War's alarms;
Let me, a peaceful Merchant, cross the Seas,
Secure to gain a fortune, and with ease.
The *Merchant*, when the threatening billows roar,
Vows he'll enlist, if once he reach the shore.   10
Far better chance he thinks at once to die,
Or triumph in the joys of Victory.

Agricolam laudat Juris legumque peritus,
Sub Galli cantum consultor ubi ostia pulsat
Ille, datis vadibus, qui rure extractus in urbem est;
Solos felices viventes clamat in urbe.
Cætera de genere hoc, adeo sunt multa, loquacem
Delassare valent Fabium........

........Ne te morer, audi
Quò rem deducam.   Si quis Deus, en ego, dicat
Jam faciam quod vultis, eris tu, qui modò miles,
Mercator: tu consultus modò, rusticus: hinc vos,
Vos hinc, mutatis discedite partibus;

The learned *Counsel*, wak'd at earlier hour,
Rises indeed, but in a temper sour,
Give me a Farm exclaims, and then for me   15
Who will may plead the Cause---nay---take the Fee.
The *Clown*, whom business up to London calls,
In gaping wonder scarce ſhall see *St. Paul's*
Before he cries, if town such joys can give,
In this fine city ever let me live.   20
The like examples, if we wanted more,
Might be produced and quoted by the score.

Jove* once thought fit with infinite good-nature
T'indulge this humour of his favourite creature;
And first, to please the Soldier,---"There's a ship,   25
" To Afric or the Indies take a trip:
" The Merchant willing to your wish will yield,
" And take your post of danger in the field.
" You Lawyer, when you like, your gown resign,
" Turn Farmer, tend your flocks and feed your swine.   30
" You Rustic, may the odious country quit,
" Dash up to town, and live the envied Cit."

.......*Eja*,

Quid! statis? Nolint.   Atqui licet esse beatus.
Quid causæ est, meritò quin illis Jupiter ambas
Iratus buccas inflet, neque se fore posthac
Tam facilem dicat, votis ut præbeat aurem?

Prætereo : ne sic, ut qui jocularia, ridens
Percurram : quanquam ridentem dicere verum
Quid vetat ? ut pueris olim dant crustula blandi
Doctores, elementa velint ut discere prima.
Sed tamen amoto quæramus seria ludo.

Illo, gravem duro terram qui vertit aratro,
Perfidus hic caupo, miles, nautæque per omne
Audaces mare qui currunt, hâc mente laborem
Sese ferre, senes ut in otia tuta recedant,
Aiunt, quum sibi sint congesta cibaria : ......

AVAR.

.......*Sicut*
Parvula (nam exemplo est) magni formica laboris

Now for the bustling change,---by gracious Heaven!
Not one accepts the offer when 'tis given.
The God, as well he might, in anger swore   35
Ne'er to regard their fickle wishes more.

But not to treat my subject as in jest,
Though truth in laughing may be well express'd,
As* oft the boy will quicker learn at school
From humorous fable, than from graver rule;   40
Jesting, however, may be out of time,
And serious things demand a serious rhyme.

Ask him, who o'er the plough, from dawn of day
Till evening dark, will bend his weary way;
Ask the brisk Tar, who dares the stormy main,   45
And quits domestic joys for distant gain;
Ask Lawyer, Soldier, What the general aim
Of their pursuits? They all reply the same:
All cry, " In toils and dangers we engage
" To gain a decent competence for age."   50

MISER.

Like,* for example's sake, the little Ant,
Who, timely guarding against future want,

Ore trahit quodcunque potest, atque addit acervo
Quem struit, haud ignara ac non incauta futuri;

HORAT.

Quæ, simul inversum contristat Aquarius annum,
Non usquam prorepit, & illis utitur ante
Quæsitis sapiens; quum te neque fervidus æstus
Demoveat lucro, neque hyems, ignis, mare, ferrum,
Nil obstet tibi, dum ne sit te ditior alter.

Quid juvat immensum te argenti pondus et auri
Furtim defossâ timidum deponere terrâ?

AVAR.

Quod, si comminuas, vellem redigatur ad assem.

Collecting as she goes, will onward creep,
And add each morsel to the rising heap.

HORACE.

Who, when she finds her labors at a stand,   55
Wisely lies by, and spends the stock in hand;
Secure, when Winter's binding frosts are o'er,
With the returning warmth of getting more.
But, Sir! is this the happy, frugal Ant,
Never to rest, yet ever live in want?   60
To bear extremes, like you, of cold and dearth,
Only to be the richest wretch on earth?
For gain,---through fire, throughs words you force your way,
Defy the rocks, and tempt the raging sea:
Nor, though the wintry storm shou'd round you roar,   65
Wou'd wish in humble safety to be poor.

Strange the enjoyment, sure, that can redound
From treasures slyly buried under ground!

MISER.

But if you touch it, once begin to spend,
Grain follows grain, and soon your heap will end.   70

HORAT.

At ni id sit, quid habet pulchri constructus acervus ?
Milia frumenti tua triverit area centum ;
Non tuus hoc capiat venter plus ac meus : ut si
Reticulum panis venales inter onusto
Forte vehas humero, nihilo plus accipias quàm
Qui nil portârit.   Vel dic, quid referat, intra
Naturæ fines viventis, jugera centum, an
Mille aret ?........

AVAR.
........At suave est de magno tollere acervo.

HORAT.
Dum ex parvo nobis tantundem haurire relinquas,
Cur tua plus laudes cumeris granaria nostris ?
Ut, tibi si sit opus liquidi non ampliùs urnâ,
Vel cyatho, ac dicas ; Magno de flumine malim
Quàm ex hoc fonticulo tantundem sumere.   Eo fit,
Plenior ut si quos delectet copia justo,

HORACE.

Truce from such monstrous reasoning, Sir ! a truce ;
For if not spend it where can be its use ?
Granted the produce of your threshing floor
Is ten times mine----but will you eat the more ?
Home from the market, and through very fear   75
Your Slave ſhou'd rob it, your own basket bear ;
Your Slave, with all the burthen thrown on you,
Will eat as much,---as much enjoy it too :
Regard indeed sufficiency alone,
And what's an hundred Acres more than one ?   80
That single Acre, if it be but mine,
Who will may plough the other ninety nine.

MISER.

Aye, but what pleasure must the thought afford,
To take, though little, from an endless hoard !

HORACE.

Leave me the measure that my wants will fill,   85
And boast the Corn of Ægypt if you will.
So if you want to drink, despise a Flask,
And beg your Landlord to produce his Cask ;
Or ſay at once, if thirsty, you'd decline
To taste a smaller current than the *Rhine* :   90

Cum ripâ simul avulsos ferat Aufidus acer:
At qui tantuli eget, quantum est opus, is neque limo
Turbatam haurit aquam, nec vitam amittit in undis.

At bona pars hominum decepta cupidine falso,
Nil satis est, inquit; quia tanti, quantum habeas, sis.
Quid facias illi? Jubeas miserum esse, libenter
Quatenus id facit: ut quidam memoratur Athenis
Sordidus ac dives, populi contemnere voces
Sic solitus: Populus me sibilat; at mihi plaudo
Ipse domi, simul ac nummos contemplor in arcâ.

Tantalus à labris sitiens fugientia captat
Flumina——Quid? rides! Mutato nomine, de te

'Tis but that passion for immoderate drink
By which so many daily drown and sink :
Who to the shallow brook resorts, no fear
Of drowning knows, and drinks his water clear.

But some, nay many, hold that no degree   95
Of Fortune upon earth too large can be ;
Because the world in general will rate
Your worth and consequence by your estate.
Now this absurd opinion what can cure ?
The Moralist must leave it to be sure :   100
Must leave such creatures to enjoy a bliss
(Since they will have it one) no more than this:
A wretch at *Athens* scarce cou'd fhew his face
In public, but was hiss'd from place to place,
" Hiss on, my Boys," he cries, " whilst I but tell   105
" The Guineas in my Closet, all is well."

Sad *Tantalus*, for ever doom'd to strain
His burning throat for water, but in vain ;---
But what, you'll say, with *Tantalus* to do ?
My Story, Sir, wou'd well apply to you :   110

D

Fabula narratur. Congestis undique saccis
Indormis inhians, et tanquam parcere sacris
Cogeris, aut pictis tanquam gaudere tabellis.

Nescis quo valeat nummus? quem præbeat usum?
Panis ematur, olus, vini sextarius; adde
Queis humana sibi doleat natura negatis.
An vigilare metu exanimem, noctesque diesque
Formidare malos fures, incendia, servos,
Ne te compilent fugientes; hoc juvat? Horum
Semper ego optârim pauperrimus esse bonorum:

AVAR.

At si condoluit tentatum frigore corpus,

Indeed the cases are so much the same,
'Tis hardly worth my while to change the name.
For what more tantalizing than to keep
The eyes wide ope that want to go to sleep?
To see the object of your wish at hand,   115
But see it——a devoted Deodand!
To grasp the Gilding, only, for the Ore!
For in your hands a Guinea is no more.

   The use of money sure you cannot know---
Buy then the comforts money will bestow;   120
Whatever hits your taste, by my advice,
If nature wants it, never stop at price.
If to be sleepless through continued fright,
Afraid of thieves by day, of fire by night,
Afraid your trustiest slave may run away   125
And with some conscious Gang divide the prey;
If these of riches are the blessings thought,
Ye Gods! may *Horace* ne'er be worth a Groat.

MISER.

But shou'd my health by accident decline,
Th' advantage then, good Sir, is clearly mine: 130

Aut alius lecto casus te adfixit; habes qui
Adsideat, fomenta paret, medicum roget, ut te
Suscitet, ac natis reddat carisque propinquis.

HORAT.

Non uxor salvum te vult, non filius; omnes
Vicini oderunt, noti, pueri, atque puellæ.
Miraris, quum tu argento post omnia ponas,
Si nemo præstet quem non merearis amorem?
At, si cognatos nullo, Natura, labore,
Quos tibi dat, retinere velis servareque amicos,
Infelix operam perdas; ut si quis asellum
In campo doceat parentem currere fræuis.

Denique sit finis quærendi: quùmque habeas plus,
Pauperiem metuas minùs; et finire laborem
Incipias, parto quod avebas: ne facias quod
Ummidius qui tam (non longa est fabula) dives

This, to keep up my spirits close attends,
That, in a hurry to the Doctor sends;
" Haste, my dear Doctor, haste to save a life,
" So dear to friends, to family, and wife."

HORACE.

Your wife, your son, your friends, so seeming civil,   135
Believe me, Sir! all wish you at the Devil;
No not a neighbour, not a child wou'd sigh,
Of all that met your funeral passing by:
And can you wonder, when to you, your Gold
Is dearer than their friendship ten times told ?   140
But if you wish to keep a needy Crew
Of Friends dependent, and your money too,
Attempt at once to ride the restive Ass,
And make him for a manag'd Courser pass:
Nay enter him to carry twenty stone,   145
And beat ECLIPSE, by all that odds to one.

In better humour now to speak, my friend
You've got enough, of getting make an end:
Nor be the character I now shall give,
Of one, you'll say, not fit on earth to live.   150

Ut metiretur nummos, ita sordidus ut se
Non unquam servo meliùs vestiret ad usque
Supremum tempus, ne se penuria victûs
Opprimeret, metuebat: at hunc liberta securi
Divisit medium, fortissima Tyndariarum.

AVAR.

Quid mí igitur suades? ut vivam Mœnius? ac sic
Ut Nomentanus?........

HORAT.

........Pergis pugnantia secum
Frontibus adversis componere. Non ego, avarum
Quum veto te fieri, vappam jubeo ac nebulonem.
Est inter Tanaïn *quiddam socerumque* Visellî.
Est modus in rebus ; sunt certi denique fines,
Quos ultra, citraque nequit consistere rectum.

Dancer,* possess'd of such enormous treasure,
That he cou'd count it only by the measure;
As if, to buy a better coat unable,
Dress'd like the meanest Ostler in a Stable;
Fear'd to the latest moment of his breath,   155
That he shou'd live to want, and starve to death.
The generous fellow, though against the laws,
Who knock'd him on the head, deserv'd applause.

MISER.

What wou'd you have me do then? Take to play,
Or make, in riot, all I have away?   160

HORACE.

This, Sir! is not to reason, but unite
Things just as opposite as black and white.
When against avarice I point my theme,
Do I advise the contrary extreme?
Who dreads the Miser's hated name to take,   165
Need not turn Spendthrift, or commence the Rake:
Sure there's a course, and easy to explore,
Betwixt an *El-w--s*, and a *B-ry-m-re*.
In all things there's a medium, from whence
Not to depart, is virtue, bliss, and sense.   170

Illuc, unde abii, redeo.   Nemon' ut avarus
Se probet, ac potiùs laudet diversa sequentes ?
Quòdque aliena capella gerat distentius uber,
Tabescat ? neque se meliori pauperiorum
Turbæ comparet ? hunc atque hunc superare laboret ?
Sic festinanti semper locupletior obstat :
Ut quum carceribus missos rapit ungula currus ;
Instat equis auriga suos vincentibus, illum
Præteritum temnens extremos inter euntem.

Inde fit, ut rarò, qui se vixisse beatum
Dicat, et exacto contentus tempore, vitâ
Cedat uti conviva satur, reperire queamus.

But* to the point again, at which I meant
To treat in general terms of discontent.
Perhaps the Miser does not stand alone,
Thus vex'd and discontented with his own ;
For do not envy and ambition's aim   175
Conduce to human misery the same ?
Is he not full as wretched who can bear
No other to succeed, no rival near ?
Despising that beneath him, all on fire
To pass the next, and get the station higher ?   180
But let him climb and labour what he will,
He sees some greater man to envy still.
Thus in the race, though only one can win,
Yet no one cares to come the second in ;
No one will cast a look behind, to see   185
The riders further from the post than he,

'Tis from these various passions, human life
Is such a scene of discontent and strife ;
From which the Actor very rare withdraws
Pleas'd, or with other's, or his own applause ;   190

D.

Jam satis est: ne me Crispini scrinia lippi
Compilâsse putes, verbum non ampliùs addam.

Scarce ever, like the satiated guest,
In humour with his day, retires to rest.

No more of this, lest haply you shou'd think
I stole, or dipp'd my pen in *Tr--sl--r's* Ink.

SAT. III. Ad M*ÆCENATEM.*

O*MNIBUS hoc vitium est cantoribus, inter amicos*
Ut nunquam inducant animum cantare rogati ;
Injussi nunquam desistant.   Sardus habebat
*Ille Tigellius hoc : C*æsar, *qui cogere posset,*
Si peteret per amicitiam patris atque suam, non
Quidquam proficeret :   Si collibuisset, ab ovo
Usque ad mala iteraret,   Iö Bacche, *modò summâ*
Voce, modò hac, resonat quæ chordis quatuor ima.

Nil æquale homini fuit illi : sæpe velut qui
Currebat fugiens hostem ; persæpe velut qui
Junonis sacra ferret : habebat sæpe ducentos,

SAT. III. To Mæcenas.

WHO with a song his friends can well amuse,
If ask'd, is almost certain to refuse ;
But take no notice---he will sit and hum,
Till you cou'd wish him in another room.
'Twas thus with *Proteus*,---urge him but to sing,   5
No ! not a single note, to please the *King :*
If in the humour,---you were hardly able
To speak, or hear each other cross the table ;
From bass to treble, high as he cou'd go,
He'd stun you with " *Hark forward! Tallio !*"   10

'Twere endless all his oddities to name,
For, life throughout, he never was the same.
Sometimes he'd run, as if the beat of drum
Announc'd that all the *Dutch* and *French* were come ;

Sæpe decem servos; modò reges atque tetrarchas,
Omnia magna loquens; modò, Sit mihi mensa tripes, et
Concha salis puri, et toga quæ defendere frigus
Quamvis crassa queat.   Decies centena dedisses
Huic parco, paucis contento, quinque diebus
Nil erat in loculis.   Noctes vigilabat ad ipsum
Mane; diem totum stertebat: Nil fuit unquam
Sic impar sibi.........

.........Nunc aliquis dicat mihi;   Quid tu?
Nullane habes vitia?   Imò alia, et fortasse minora.

Then halt, and settle on a pace so slow　　　　　15
As scarce wou'd follow up a funeral shew.
To day---ten footman smart in livery suits,
To morrow---not a boy to clean his boots;
To day---of knowing kings and princes vain,
To morrow---talking in this altered strain;　　20
" Give me but bread and cheese, far better fare,
" Than living with a prince, or prince's heir:
" And as for coat, it matters not how old
" Or coarse, if 'twill but fence against the cold."
With all this temperance, in three days hence　　25
A thousand pounds wou'd dwindle down to pence.
For times and seasons, 'twas his great delight,
To change the order of the day and night;
All night awake, and sitting up at play;
Supine asleep and snoring all the day.　　　　30
There never was, and never will, I ween,
Be such an inconsistent creature seen.

　Now some may ask, and with much justice too,
" And, pray Sir! are there then no faults in you ? "
Yes--- perhaps, many; and my stars I'll bless,　35
If, in comparison, they shou'd be less.

Mænius *absentem* Novium *quum carperet : Heus tu!*
Quidam ait, ignoras te? an ut ignotum dare nobis
Verba putas? Egomet mî ignosco, Mænius *inquit.*

Stultus et improbus hic amor est, dignusque notari.
Quùm tua prætereas oculis malè lippus inunctis,
Cur in amicorum vitiis tam cernis acutum,
Quàm aut aquila, aut serpens Epidaurius? At tibi contra
Evenit, inquirant vitia ut tua rursus et illi.

Iracundior est paulò ; minùs aptus acutis
Naribus horum hominum : rideri possit, eo quòd
Rusticiùs tonso toga defluit, et malè laxus

Mænius, his absent friend must scandalize ;---
" Hold," cries another, " open your own eyes ;
" Are you so perfect, that you find no room
" For blame or censure, when you look at home ?"   40
Mænius, (that such a character shou'd live !)
Replies,---" My own defects, Sir ! I forgive."

This partial judgment is a grand offence
'Gainst candour, decency, and common sense :
For tell me, when you look with eye askew,   45
And your own faults indeed will hardly view ;
Into your neighbour's shou'd you pry so far,
And strain your sight, like *Herschel* at a star ?
No, Sir ! nor is it prudent in the main,
For they will look as sharp at you again.   50

Your friend, perhaps, can hardly stand a jest,
Or goes, we'll say, too negligently dress'd :
So careless, that you can but smile to see
Buckles, in make and metal disagree ;
Unshav'd, unpowder'd, and in such a coat,   55
You well may doubt if made for him or not ;

F

In pede calceus hæret. At est bonus, ut melior vir
Non alius quisquam ; at tibi amicus ; at ingenium ingens
Inculto latet hoc sub corpore........

........Denique teipsum
Concute, num qua tibi vitiorum inseverit olim
Natura, aut etiam consuetudo mala : namque
Neglectis urenda filix innascitur agris.

Illuc prævertamur, amatorem quòd amicæ
Turpia decipiunt cæcum vitia, aut etiam ipsa hæc
Delectant; veluti Balbinum polypus Hagnæ.
Vellem in amicitiâ sic erraremus, et isti
Errori nomen Virtus possuisset honestum.

At, pater ut nati, sic nos debemus amici,
Si quod sit vitium, non fastidire. Strabonem

You laugh again, and wonder how he goes
In such a loose, ill fitting pair of shoes.
But who then is he?---Why, a better man
You'll never find, look for him where you can :   60
Of first rate sense---and, more to recommend,
To you, a generous and a steady friend.

    Examine then yourself---perhaps you'll find
Nature, in some things, has not been too kind :
But at the best, you fairly may expect   65
To find some faults arising from neglect :
For slack the tillage that your field requires,
And the rank soil produces weeds and briars.

    The shorter method and the best, may prove,
To see as partial, as we see in Love ;   70
Where* to the gentle loving *Strephon's* eye
A little twist is no deformity :
In friendship but admit the same mistake,
What firm and lasting friendships wou'd it make !

    But let us copy (for that is not hard)   75
The partial judgment of the *Sire's* regard :

Appellat Pœtum pater; et Pullum malè parvus
Si cui filius est, ut abortivus fuit olim
Sisyphus; hunc Varum, distortis cruribus: illum
Balbutit Scaurum, talis fultum malè pravis.

Parcius hic vivit: frugi dicatur.   Ineptus
Et jactantior hic paulò est; concinnus amicis
Postulat ut videatur.   At est truculentior, atque
Plus æquo liber; simplex fortisque habeatur.
Caldior est; acres inter numeretur.   Opinor,
Hæc res et jungit, junctos et servat amicos.

At nos virtutes *ipsas invertimus, atque*

Has he a Son that looks too much awry?
" 'Tis but a pleasing archness in his eye."
Is he like *Borowlaski*, short and small?
" 'Tis true the pretty poppet is not tall."   80
If bandy legg'd,----" He's not exactly strait."
Whole footed,----" Rather awkward in his gait."

So for ourselves,----If chance our friend should be,
In parting with his money not so free;
To put this best construction let us try,---   85
" He has his motives for œconomy."
Does he love boasting? crack a silly jest?
" He means to entertain, and 'tis his best."
But he is blunt: Say 'tis dislike of art,
And the plain frankness of an honest heart.   90
Is he too choleric? " Oh no, 'tis spirit;
" For after all, good nature is his merit."
Thus shou'd we gain and keep our friends with ease,
Pleas'd both with them, and sure ourselves to please.

But we, oh shame! with base inverted mind   95
Even with *virtues* strive our faults to find.

Sincerum cupimus vas incrustare.   Probus quis
Nobiscum vivit, multùm demissus homo: illi
Tardo ac cognomen pingui damus.   Hic fugit omnes
Insidias, nullique malo latus obdit apertum,
Quum genus hoc inter vitæ versemur, (ubi acris
Invidia, atque vigent ubi crimina,) pro bene sano
Ac non incauto, fictum astutumque vocamus.
Simplicior quis et est, (qualem me sæpe libenter
Obtulerim tibi, Mæcenas,) ut fortè legentem,
Aut tacitum appellet quovis sermone molestus;
Communi sensu planè caret, inquimus........

........Eheu!
Quàm temerè in nosmet legem sancimus iniquam!
Nam vitiis nemo sine nascitur: optimus ille est,
Qui minimis urgetur........

And, whilst with envy's jaundic'd eyes we view,
Make the bright object look discolor'd too.
Lives there a man, of conduct just and right,
But of abilities not over bright;   100
Modest, or much reserv'd---we join at once
To call him lifeless and unmeaning dunce.
Lives there another, of abundant care
To shun the villainous *Informer's* snare;
(And 'faith the present traiterous times are such   105
You cannot be upon your guard too much)
In him, who thus but acts a prudent part,
We see suspicion vile, and deep laid art.
Shou'd the poor *Vicar*, or the *Man of Rhyme*
Call on his *Patron* at improper time;   110
Tho' neither meant to give the least offence,
'Tis deemed at once, a want of common sense.

Alas! how ready to invent and make
The very laws which we ourselves must break:
For no one lives, but shares in some degree   115
The faults and follies of humanity.
Happy the man!---yes, happiest he and best,
Not, who is sinless,---but, who sins the least.

..........*Amicus dulcis, ut æquum est,*
Cum mea compenset vitiis bona, pluribus hisce
(Si modò plura mihi bona sunt) inclinet, amari
Si volet: hac lege in trutinâ ponetur câdem.
Qui, ne tuberibus propriis offendat amicum,
Postulat; ignoscet verrucis illius.   Æquum est
Peccatis veniam poscentem reddere rursus.

Denique, quatenus excidi penitus vitium iræ,
Cætera item nequeunt stultis hærentia; cur non
Ponderibus modulisque suis ratio *utitur? ac, res*
Ut quæque est, ita suppliciis delicta coërcet?
Si quis eum servum, patinam qui tollere jussus
Semesos pisces tepidumque ligurierit jus,
In cruce suffigat; Labeone insanior inter
Sanos dicatur.   Quantò hoc furiosìus, atque
Majus peccatum est? paulùm deliquit amicus;

But let my friend, it is but justice due,
Weigh both my vices and my virtues too :   120
And shou'd my virtues happily prevail,
Approve me in the meritorious scale :
On this condition, he is sure to see
The same indulgent temper reign in me.
Who hopes his own defects may not offend,   125
Must wave defects inherent in his friend ;
And, if we wish in harmony to live,
Who wants allowance, must allowance give.

But after all, 'tis past our power we find
To root out angry passions from the mind :   130
Let REASON then her equal scales produce,
And regulate her laws by human use.
Shou'd you the boy, who, carrying off the dish,
Presum'd to taste a morsel of the fish,
Kill in a passion,----take it for a rule,   135
The world wou'd call you madman or a fool.
Now how much nearer to the man of sense
Are you, so ready on the least offence
To shun your friend, and cruelly resent
Affronts, most likely, that he never meant ;   140

G

Quod nisi concedas, habeare insuavis ; acerbus
Odisti et fugis, ut Rusonem debitor æris ;
Qui nisi, quùm tristes misero venere Calendæ,
Mercedem aut nummos unde unde extricat, amaras
Porrecto jugulo historias, captivus ut, audit.

Comminxit lectum potus ; mensáve catillum
Evandri manibus tritum dejecit ; ob hanc rem,
Aut positum ante meâ quia pullum in parte catini
Sustulit esuriens, minùs hoc jucundus amicus
Sit mihi ? Quid faciam, furtum si fecerit, aut si
Prodiderit commissa fide, sponsumve negarit ?

Queis paria esse ferè placuit peccata, laborant,
Cùm ventum ad verum est : sensus moresque repugnant,
Atque ipsa utilitas, justi prope mater et æqui.

Look with reserve, in haste his presence quit,
As if he came to serve a *Sheriff's* writ:
Avoid him, as the fearful debtor shuns
His *scribbling* creditor, who worse than duns;
For, if he fails in payment at the day,   145
Condemn'd he sits to hear him read his *play*.

My friend had drank too much, and rose, 'twas said,
From damper sheets, than when he went to bed;
At breakfast, blundered down a china bowl,
Which breaks a favorite set, and spoils the whole;   150
At dinner, in the strangest hungry way,
Snatch'd both my chicken and my plate away:
Such trifling things as these, Sir! shall I deem
Sufficient faults, to lessen my esteem?
Had he broke ope, and pillag'd my 'scrutore,   155
Broke his most solemn vows---I cou'd no more.

Who for *equality* of crimes contend,
Cannot support their doctrine to the end;
'Tis against sense, and be it understood,
The maxim is against the public good.   160

Cùm prorepserunt primis animalia terris,
Mutum ac turpe pecus, glandem atque cubilia propter,
Unguibus et pugnis, dein fustibus, atque ita porro
Pugnabant armis, quæ post fabricaverat usus:
Donec verba, quibus voces sensusque notarent,
Nominaque invenere: dehinc absistere bello,
Oppida cœperunt munire, et ponere leges,
Ne quis fur esset, neu latro, neu quis adulter.
Nam fuit ante Helenam Mulier teterrima belli
Causa: sed ignotis perierunt mortibus illi,
Quos Venerem incertam rapientes more ferarum
Viribus editior cædebat, ut in grege taurus.

What time the race of mortals after birth,
Crept from the cradle of their parent earth,
But little better than the brutes they rose
And settl'd right and property by blows.
At first with fists and claws, their weapons rude,   165
They fought for caves and for their acorn food :
Next clubs were us'd, 'till more progressive art
Produc'd the sword, the spear, and missile dart :
A nobler science, after ages teach,
Gave birth to words, and cloath'd their thoughts with speech:
Hence ripening wisdom bade contention cease,
Erected towns, and taught the arts of peace :
Then laws were fram'd, the thief and murderer's dread,
And justice guarded the connubial bed.
For long ere *Helen*, Woman's fatal charms   175
Embroil'd the world and set mankind in arms ;
The weaker Lover sunk beneath the strong,
But died unnotic'd---for he died unsung ;
Whilst, like the lowing herds, in fields and groves,
The wand'ring Savage sought promiscuous loves.   180

   Whoe'er ascending back, from age to age,
Explores the records of th' historic page,

Jura inventa metu injusti fateare necesse est,
Tempora si fastosque velis evolvere mundi.
Nec Natura potest justo secernere iniquum,
Dividit ut bona diversis, fugienda petendis :
Nec vincet ratio hoc, tantumdem ut peccet idemque,
Qui teneros caules alieni fregerit horti,
Et qui nocturnus sacra Divûm legerit........

..........Adsit
Regula, peccatis quæ pœnas irroget æquas :
Ne scuticâ dignum horribili sectere flagello.
Nam, ut feruld cædas meritum majora subire
Verbera, non vereor ; quum dicas esse pares res
Furta latrociniis ; et magnis parva mineris
Falce recisurum simili te, si tibi regnum
Permittant homines........

This sure conclusion from his search must draw,
That fear of wrong, at first gave rise to Law :
And though, by nature's light, we well descry   185
What things we ought to follow, what to fly ;
We never can, by simple nature's light,
Distinguish justice from its opposite ;
And reason never can convince me still,
Reason as close and shrewdly as you will,   190
That the poor boy, who chance shall break a hedge,
To steal an apple---commits sacrilege.

In short, your laws with justice to dispense,
Proportion keep 'twixt law and the offence ;
Nor let the culprit, who deserves to feel   195
The beadle's lash, be broke upon the wheel.
That you shou'd ease his penalties or pains,
I need not fear, if you shou'd hold the reins ;
Since in degrees of crimes, or great or small,
You don't allow a difference at all ;   200
Vow, if the nation wou'd but make you king,
Who murders, or who robs, alike shou'd swing.

........*Si dives, qui sapiens est,*
Et sutor bonus, et solus formosus, et est rex;
Cur optas quod habes? Non nôsti quid pater, inquit,
Chrysippus *dicat*; *Sapiens crepidas sibi numquam*
Nec soleas fecit: sutor tamen est sapiens.

HORAT.

Qui?

STOIC.

Ut, quamvis tacet Hermogenes, *cantor tamen atque*
Optimus est modulator; *ut* Alfenus *vafer, omni*
Abjecto instrumento artis, clausáque tabernâ,
Tonsor erat; *sapiens operis sic optimus omnis*
Est opifex solus,---sic rex.........

But why the wish ?   If what you say be true,
Already, every inch a king are you.
The wise man, so your doctrine seems to say,   205
Is rich, though for his coat he cannot pay :
The wise man, if I understand the thing,
You hold to be both Cobler and a King.
But you contend, your favorite bent to praise,
I quite mistake what sage *Chrysippus* says ;   210
For though the wise man does not keep the shop,
Still of the *Crispins* he may be the top.
Your reasoning is too subtle for my brain,
So, if you please, good Sir ! the sense explain.

STOIC.

'Tis* thus---Though *Siddons* from the house shou'd stay, 215
She's our first Actress, though she does not play :
Alike the *Pall-mall* Cobler, who of late
Left mending Shoes, to vamp and botch the State ;
Call him Reformer, Patriot, what you will,
Is but a Cobler, and a poor one still.   220
The wise man thus, may call himself a King,
A Cobler, Barber, Taylor, any thing.

HORAT.

.........Vellunt tibi barbam
Lascivi pueri, quos tu nisi fuste coërces,
Urgeris turbâ circùm te stante, miserque
Rumperis et latras, magnorum maxime regum.

Ne longum faciam; dum tu quadrante lavatum
Rex ibis, neque te quisquam stipator, ineptum
Præter Crispinum, sectabitur; et mihi dulces
Ignoscent, si quid peccâro stultus, amici;
Inque vicem illorum patiar delicta libenter,
Privatusque magis vivam te rege beatus.

HORACE.

Still I suspect, thou mighty *Stoic* prince!
The boys may pluck your beard, and make you wince!
Yes, pluck that reverend beard, unless your stick   225
Shou'd make the urchins of their frolick sick;
Whilst the surrounding mob enjoy the fun,
Encourage the attack, and cry " Well done."

Whilst you, dread Sir! shall to your cellar go
And rule your penny club, a king below;   230
Let me my friend's defects with temper see,
And they the same indulgence shew to me;
Then, private as I am, I'll happier live
Than you, with all that Majesty can give.

S A T.   IX.

IBAM *fortè viâ sacrâ (sicut meus est mos)*
Nescio quid meditans nugarum, totus in illis :
Accurrit quidam notus mihi nomine tantùm,
Arreptâque manu : Quid agis, dulcissime rerum ?
Suaviter, ut nunc est, inquam : et cupio omnia quæ vis.
Quum assectaretur : Numquid vis ? occupo.   *At ille :*
Nôris nos, inquit : docti sumus.   Hic ego, Pluris
Hoc, *inquam,* mihi eris. ....

S A T.   IX.

AMUS'D, as usual, in my morning walk
With trifling thoughts, and to myself in talk;
Not quite a Stranger, for I knew his name,
And that was all, abrupt upon me came:
Seizes my hand---" My dearest Sir! what you ?   5
" Well, I rejoice to see you, how d'ye do ? "
Why, for the present, happy in the main;
And, Sir! I wish as much to you again.
When he still follow'd close, I cou'd but say---
Business of any kind with me this way ?   10
" No, Sir! not any;---what you know so well,
" That I'm a Critic, is no news to tell."
A Critic !---then upon the Critic's score,
I cannot but respect your person more.

........*Miserè discedere quærens,*
Ire modò ociùs, interdum consistere, in aurem
Discere nescio quid puero. *Quum sudor ad imos*
Manaret talos: O te, Bolane, *cerebri*
Felicem! aiebam tacitus. ....

........*Quum quidlibet ille*
Garriret: vicos, urbem laudaret; Ut illi
Nil respondebam: Miserè cupis, inquit; abire;
Jamdudum video: sed nil agis: usque tenebo.
Prosequar hinc, quò nunc iter est tibi. Nil opus est te
Circumagi; quendam volo visere non tibi notum;
Trans Tiberim longè cubat is, prope Cæsaris hortos.

Anxious above all measure to get clear,   15
I whisper'd something in my Servant's ear;
One minute ran, another, almost stood,
To leave, or let him pass me, if he wou'd:
But all in vain---without remorse he prates,
Praises the Town, the Churches, and the Streets;   20
'Till quite worn out with his eternal talk,
And sweating with vexation and my walk,
Oh! how I long'd to tell him what I thought,
And speak like Dr. *Johnson** to a *Scot.*

To all his chat, so trifling and absurd,   25
When he perceiv'd I answer'd not a word,
" Come, my good Sir!" says he; " I plainly see
" You want to leave me most confoundedly;
" But not a step without me,---I'll attend
" And see you safely at your journey's end."   30
Your most obedient;--but, good Sir! I pray
Don't let me take you so much from your way:
I have to cross the River, and beside
May have to wait the rising of the Tide;
My friend then lives a mile and half, or two,   35
Up in the Country, and unknown to you.

Nil habeo quod agam, et non sum piger; usque sequar te.
Demitto auriculas, ut iniquæ mentis asellus,
Quum gravius dorso subiit onus. ....

.........*Incipit ille :*
Si bene me novi, non Viscum *pluris amicum,*
Non Varium *facies : nam quis me scribere plures,*
Aut citiùs possit versus ? quis membra movere
Molliùs ? Invideat quod et Hermogenes, *ego canto.*

Interpellandi locus hic erat. Est tibi mater,
Cognati, queis te salvo est opus ? *Haud mihi quisquam :*
Omnes composui. ....

" As for the distance, Sir,---I'm quite at leisure;
" To wait is nothing, and the walk 's a pleasure."
No Ass o'erloaded with both panniers full,
Cou'd hang his ears, more vicious or more dull.   40

    " If I mistake not, Sir, in me you'll find,
" Exactly the companion to your mind.
" In solid sense, or livelier flights of wit
" A match for *Fox*, for *Sheridan*, or *Pitt* :
" If numberless and hasty verses shew it,   45
" *Peter* himself is not a better poet :
" Of other graces, *dancing* is my forte,
" In which I yield to no one Lord at court ;
" And for a *song*, I'll venture to engage,
" I beat the finest voice on either stage."   50

    'Twas an odd question truly---but my man
Here made a moment's pause, and I began.
Pray, Sir ! no mother, family, or friends,
Whose welfare on your health perhaps depends ?
" No, thanks to Heaven ! not a living soul---   55
" The one I burried last, wound up the whole."

........*Felices ! nunc ego resto ;*
Confice : namque instat fatum mihi triste; Sabella
Quod puero cecinit motâ divina anus urnâ :
Hunc neque dira venena, neque hosticus auferet ensis,
Nec laterum dolor, aut tussis, nec tarda podagra ;
Garrulus *hunc quando consumet cunque : loquaces,*
Si sapiat, vitet, simul atque adoleverit ætas.

Ventum erat ad Vestæ, *quartâ jam parte diei*
Præteritâ ; et casu tunc respondere vadatus
Debebat ; quòd nî fecisset, perdere litem.
Si me amas, inquit, paulùm hìc ades. Interearn, si
Aut valeo stare, aut novi civilia jura :
Et propero, quò scis. *Dubius sum quid faciam, inquit ;*
Tene relinquam, an rem. Me sodes. ....

Oh, happy they! thought I; 'tis all I crave,
In mercy now dispatch me to my grave!
Now comes the fate a *Gypsy* once foreshew'd,
When yet a child I rambl'd to *Norwood*. 60
This Boy, said she, as she my palm explor'd,
Is safe from halters, poisons, and the sword;
No pains from pleurisy, no bursting cough,
Or crippling gout shall ever take him off:
But in his *Line of Death* a *Talker* lies, 65
Of age, he'll shun all Talkers, if he's wise.

We now were passing opposite *Guild-hall*,
Ten had just finish'd striking by St. *Paul*,
Where, as good luck wou'd have it, he was bound
To stand a suit, or forfeit fifty pound. 70
" Step, my dear Sir, one minute into Court,
" (The trial, I engage, will be but short)
" And I may thank you."----*Sir! I nothing know
Of Courts, and, as you see, am hurry'd too.*
" I feel myself now fairly on the pause, 75
" Whether to give up you, or leave my cause."
*Oh me, no doubt---no doubt, Sir, can remain,
And so---your humble servant once again.*

........*Non faciam, ille;*
Et præcedere cœpit.   Ego, ut contendere durum
Cum victore, sequor. ....

........*Mæcenas quomodo tecum?*
(Hinc repetit;) Paucorum hominum et mentis bene sanæ.
Nemo dexteriùs fortunâ est usus: haberes
Magnum adjutorem, posset qui ferre secundas;
Hunc hominem velles si tradere; dispeream, ni
Summôsses omnes. ....

........Isto non vivitur illic,
Quo tu rere, modo.   Domus hac nec purior ulla est,

" Well, hang the business---finish as it will,
" I'll keep with you my last engagement still." 80
Fairly knock'd up, and nothing more to say,
I follow now just where he leads the way.

Again his nonsense I am doom'd to hear---
" Well, Sir! how stand you with our *Minister ?*"
Sir, he's a man of sense---but rather close, 85
Likes but few friends, and very choice in those.
" If once to play with Ministers I get,
" Few men, perhaps, more seldom lose a hit;
" And what I value most in all my art,
" I play, as well as first, a second part. 90
" Hang me, if 'twou'd not answer well your end
" To introduce me to him, as your friend :
" With my assistance, I'll be bound you clear
" The coast, and soon monopolize his ear."

Sir, you mistake---mistake the matter much ; 95
The mode of living there is no ways such :
Search the whole City, and you'll hardly see
A house from such disorders stands more free.

Nec magis his aliena malis : nîl mî officit, inquam,
Ditior hic, aut est quia doctior : est locus uni-
Cuique suus. ....

........*Magnum narras, vix credibile.* Atqui
Sic habet. ....

........*Accendis quare cupiam magis illi*
Proximus esse. Velis tantummodo, quæ tua virtus,
Expugnabis : et est qui vinci possit ; eòque
Difficiles aditus primos habet. *Haud mihi deero :*
Muneribus servos corrumpam ; non, hodie si
Exclusus fuero, desistam : ....

I never find a difference between
*Myself, or any L*ORD *that may come in :*　　　　　100
He knows, but never bears on me so hard,
As to say PETER *is the better Bard :*
Each has his proper place, and each receives
The due respect his proper station gives.

"Sir, you surprize---our Minister is this?"　　　105
Sir, you may be surpriz'd---but so it is.

"You fire my inclinations still the more
"To know your worthy patron than before."
Well, Sir, you need but wish it---for once known,
Merit like yours must introduce alone ;　　　　110
To worth he nothing can at last deny,
And from a sense of this, at first is shy.
"If that's the case, depend upon 't I'll spare
"No kind of pains to get admission there ;
"If gold will do---as far as money goes　　　　115
"In bribing Servants, they shall have their dose.
"Shou'd *John*, with door half open, coolly say,
"My Master, Sir, is not at home to day ;

..........*Tempora quæram;*

Occurram in triviis : deducam.   Nil sine magno
Vita labore dedit mortalibus. ....

...........*Hæc dum agit; ecce*
Fuscus Aristius *occurrit, mihi carus, et illum*
Qui pulchrè nosset.   Consistimus.   Unde venis? et
Quò tendis? rogat, et respondet.   Vellere cæpi,
Et prensare manu lentissima brachia, nutans,
Distorquens oculos, ut me eriperet.   Malè salsus
Ridens dissimulare : meum jecur urere bilis.
Certè nescio quid secretò velle loqui te
Aiebas mecum.   *Memini bene; sed meliori*
Tempore dicam; hodie tricesima sabbata.   Vis tu
Curtis Judæis *oppedere?* ....

" I'll go the next---watch all occasions, plan
" All schemes to shew myself his partizan ;   120
" Attend his levees ; and if he goes out,
" Be foremost in huzzaing him about.
" Nothing of moment since the world begun,
" Without great labor ever yet was done."

   Just at this crisis, who shou'd come in view
But my friend *Fuscus*, who the fellow knew ;
" What?---For a walk."---He asks and answers too.
Instant I try to squeeze him by the hand,
Attempt by nods to make him understand ;
But not a signal will he see, or feel ;   130
I might as well attempt to hold an eel :
The Rogue but laughs, my awkward state to see,
Whilst what is laugh to him, is death to me.
Sir, when we took our leave the other day,
Something, not thought of then, you had to say.   135
" I well remember, but, if not a crime,
" For business this is not a proper time.
" 'Tis the Jew's Sabbath ; and you wou'd not chuse,
" Whate'er their customs, to offend the *Jews* ? "

K

........Nulla mihi, *inquam,*
Religio est.   *At mi; sum paulò infirmior, unus*
Multorum; ignosces: aliàs loquar. ....

........*Hunccine solem*
Tam nigrum surrêxe mihi?   Fugit improbus, ac me
Sub cultro linquit. ....

........*Casu venit obvius illi*
Adversarius; et, quò tu turpissime? magnâ
Inclamat voce, et, Licet antestari?   Ego verò
Oppono auriculam.   Rapit in jus; clamor utrimque,
Undique concursus.   Sic me servavit Apollo.

'Faith Sir, I have no such scruples about me---   140
" But Sir ! I have, to tell you honestly :
" Call my religion weak, or over-fervent,
" 'Tis my religion---so, your humble servant."

Oh ! that so dark a Sun shou'd ever rise !
In cruel sport away the creature flies ;   145
And leaves his friend, half worried out of life,
To the last cut and struggle with the knife.

The Plaintiff now came up in raging bile,
Collar'd, and call'd him every thing that's vile :
" Sir ! will you bear me witness, that 'tis he,   150
" The very Rogue I want ? " *most willingly.*
Instant he drags the Culprit into Court ;
Loud clamours rise from tongues of every sort ;
I walk in quiet off---and thank APOLLO for't.

LIBER SECUNDUS.

SAT. V.

ULYSSES.   TIRESIAS.

ULYSSES.

HOC quoque, Tiresia, præter narrata, petenti
Responde: quibus amissas reparare queam res
Artibus atque modis?   Quid rides? ....

TIRESIAS.

........Jamne, dolose,
Non satis est Ithacam revehi, patriosque penates
Aspicere? ....

ULYSSES.

........O nulli quidquam mentite, vides ut

SECOND BOOK,

SAT. V.

ULYSSES. TIRESIAS.

ULYSSES.

THIS once, Tiresias, and but this I ask,
Resume your friendly and prophetic task:
How shall I act, my fortunes to repair,
So shatter'd and to pieces as they are?

TIRESIAS.

How now, sly Pilgrim!---To your country get,   5
Your native home---and not contented yet?

ULYSSES.

Prophet of Truth!---so far I own to thee
Myself in debt,---but what is home to me?

Nudus inopsque domum redeo, te vate : neque illic
Aut apotheca procis intacta est, aut pecus.   Atqui
Et genus et virtus, nisi cum re, vilior algâ est.

TIRESIAS.

Quando pauperiem, missis ambagibus, horres :
Accipe, quâ ratione queas ditescere.   Turdus,
Sive aliud privum dabitur tibi : devolet illuc,
Res ubi magna nitet, domino sene : dulcia poma,
Et quoscunque feret cultus tibi fundus honores,
Ante Larem gustet venerabilior Lare dives.
Qui quamvis perjurus erit, sine gente, cruentus
Sanguine fraterno, fugitivus ; ne tamen illi
Tu comes exterior, si postulet, ire recuses.

ULYSSES.

Utne tegam spurco Damæ latus ? Haud ita Trojæ
Me gessi, certans semper melioribus. ....

Stripp'd, as you see me, by a set of Wooers,
My goods, and house itself turn'd out of doors?   10
And what is worth, or name, however grand,
Without a single shilling at command?

TIRESIAS.

Since poverty 's the ail you can't endure,
Take this receipt---I'll answer for the cure.
A *Woodcock*, let us say, by chance is sent   15
To you, or to your Wife a compliment;
No matter which---for, instant let it fly
A present to some rich old neighbour nigh.
To him the choicest produce of your fields;
To him the choicest fruits your garden yields: 20
What though your houshold Gods you thus deprive?
He is the God for you, who most can give.
Your God well knows the pillory, 'tis true,
For various crimes---but what is that to you?
For such disgraces, never less attend,   25
Or blush, if he approves, to call him friend.

ULYSSES.

ULYSSES act a character so low,
Whose pride through life, has ever been to shew

TIRESIAS.

..........Ergo

Pauper eris. ....

ULYSSES.

........Fortem hoc animum tolerare jubebo ;
Et quondam majori tuli.   Tu protinus, unde
Divitias ærisque ruam, dic augur, acervos.

TIRESIAS.

Dixi equidem, et dico.   Captes astutus ubique
Testamenta senum : neu, si vafer unus et alter
Insidiatorem præroso fugerit hamo,
Aut spem deponas, aut artem illusus omittas.

Magna minorve foro si res certabitur olim ;

A spirit, daring above meaner things,
To stand at once pre-eminent of Kings !   30

TIRESIAS.

If such your spirit still---I say no more---
Your pride, good Sir ! must ever keep you poor.

ULYSSES.

So let it then :---if such the means to thrive,
Poor and distress'd as ever, let me live.
Some other method, mark'd with less disgrace,   35
Propose, my scatter'd fortunes to replace.

TIRESIAS.

I told you once, and tell you now once more,
No way so good, as what I nam'd before.
But---find some wealthy merchant, old or ill,
And set your traps to catch him in his will :   40
Nor be dismay'd, if one or two, or more,
Elude the hook too thinly cover'd o'er ;
Off to another, nor the hope forsake,
That the next better baited hook may take.

Again---suppose a cause is to be tried,---   45
Never enquire the merits of each side,

Vivet uter locuples sine natis, improbus; ultro
Qui meliorem audax vocet in jus, illius esto
Defensor : famâ civem causâque priorem
Sperne, domi si natus erit, fecundave conjux.

Quinte, puta, aut Publi (gaudent prænomine molles
Auriculæ) tibi me virtus tua fecit amicum :
Jus anceps novi : causas defendere possum :
Eripiet quivis oculos citius mihi, quàm te
Contentum cassâ nuce pauperet : hæc mea cura est,
Ne quid tu perdas, neu sis jocus.   Ire domum atque
Pelliculam curare jube : si cognitor ipse :
Persta, atque obdura : seu rubra canicula findet
Infantes statuas ; seu pingui tentus omaso
Furius hybernas canâ nive conspuet Alpes.

Or ask which character the best may be,
But which can give the best *retaining Fee.*
Defend with all your might his viler cause,
And leave the worthier client to the laws.   50
RIGHT is with him---'tis granted---but, ods'life,
The man has heirs, and still a breeding wife.

    Now for address; your titles never spare,
(Titles are winning to a scoundrel's ear,)
" Most noble Sir ! your worth has long ago   55
" Acquired you the esteem I wish to shew.
" I know the laws, and know the case in hand,
" But leave it all to me, for understand
" No living soul shall rob you of your due,
" Which, I aver, is costs and damage too: 60
" Go home, sweet Sir ! and leave your cares with me."
And now with all dispatch put in your plea:
Push into Court, tho' *Sirius* shou'd throw
A heat, that splits the pavement as you go;
Or* great *Dubartas* bridle up the Floods,   65
And periwig with snow the bald pate woods.
Quote dubious cases, then descend to sport,
This to mislead, and that t' amuse the Court;

Nonne vides (aliquis cubito stantem prope tangens
Inquiet) ut patiens, ut amicis aptus, ut acer ?
.Plures adnabunt thynni, et cetaria crescent.

Si cui præterea validus malè filius in re
Præclarâ sublatus aletur; ne manifestum
Cælibis *obsequium nudet te, leniter in spem*
Arrepe officiosus, ut et scribare secundus
Heres, *et si quis casus puerum egerit Orco,*
In vacuum venias. Perrarò hæc alea fallit.

Qui testamentum tradet tibi cunque legendum,

'Till, all amaz'd and charm'd, the standers by
Exclaim, what wondrous sense ! what energy !　　70
With such an active counsel for his friend,
Who needs suspect a verdict in the end ?
Your name is up,---you now may raise your fees,
And pick and chuse your clients as you please :
Nay, if you like it, what few counsel can,　　75
May plead for RIGHT alone, and be an honest man.

　　Let us, again, suppose an only son,
(To blind your views on *Batchelors* alone)
So puny, that the faculty give out
The hapless youth can never come about :　　80
Here 's a fine opening, manage it with skill,
To stand the *second* in the Father's will :
And shou'd the darling brat his breath resign,
House, lands and tenements, may all be thine.
This for an heirship, (when there 's no *entail)*　　85
Is the best chance, and seldom known to fail.

　　Another, in much confidence, requests,
" Pray look at this,---how like you my bequests ?"

Abnuere, et tabulas â te removere memento:
Sic tamen, ut limis rapias, quid prima secundo
Cera velit versu; solus multisne coheres,
Veloci percurre oculo. Plerumque recoctus
Scriba ex quinqueviro corvum deludet hiantem;
Captatorque dabit risus Nasica Corano.

U L Y S S E S.

Num furis? an prudens ludis me, obscura canendo?

T I R E S I A S.

O Laërtiade, *quidquid dicam, aut erit, aut non:*
Divinare etenim magnus mihi donat Apollo.

U L Y S S E S.

Quid tamen ista velit sibi fabula, si licet, ede.

Be sure refuse, with " Sir ! no doubt a true,
" A just and honest will, if made by you."   90
With all this negligence, make sure to see,
At a side glance, where you stand legatee.
But this advice, in general good indeed,
May not, in every case you try, succeed :
Some deeper head may see your cunning through,   95
And turn at last, the tables upon you ;
As will *Nasica*, be at length the fool
To him, of whom he means to make a tool.

ULYSSES.

Nasica ! speak you now my reverend sage,
In banter, or in true prophetic rage ?   100

TIRESIAS.

Laertes' son ! whatever I portend
Or will---or will not---happen in the end ;
For thus, of prophets the great god and king,
Has taught, divinely taught, his priest to sing.

ULYSSES.

Then, if the mighty secret may be told,   105
The sequel of your mystic tale unfold.

TIRESIAS.

Tempore quo juvenis Parthis *horrendus ab alto*
Demissum genus Æneâ, tellure marique
Magnus erit ; forti nubet procera Corano
Filia Nasicæ, *metuentis reddere soldum.*
Tum gener hoc faciet : tabulas socero dabit, atque
Ut legat orabit ; multùm Nasica *negatas*
Accipiet tandem ; tacitus leget, invenietque
Nil sibi legatum, præter plorare, suisque.

Illud ad hæc jubeo : mulier si fortè dolosa,
Libertusve senem delirum temperet ; illis
Accedas socius : laudes, lauderis ut absens.
Adjuvat hoc quoque : sed vincit longè prius ipsum
Expugnare caput. ....

TIRESIAS.

What time a youth, the *Parthian's* dread, whose line
From great *Æneas* boasts its race divine,
By land and sea shall triumph,---will be led
Nasica's daughter to *Coranus'* bed :   110
So hopes the *Sire* his creditor to gull
Of a good jointure and receipt in full.
Then shall the sated letcher, craftier still,
Entreat *Nasica* to peruse his will :
Long shall he hesitate,---at length obey,   115
Read it in silence, and, in dire dismay,
Find at the last, deluded in his turn,
Himself and child left nothing,---but to mourn.

An artful girl, again, shall have the rule
Of some old driv'ling, love distracted fool :   120
Or chance his servant shall be master grown,
Dispose and order all things as his own.
To form a close connexion here, be sure ;
Praise, of their praises, when you're gone, secure.
But after all, the surest path to tread,   125
Is that which leads directly to the *head :*

M

..........Scribet mala carmina vecors ?
Laudato. Scortator erit ? cave te roget : ultro
Penelopen *facilis potiori trade*. ....

ULYSSES.

........Putasne,
Perduci poterit tam frugi tamque pudica,
Quam nequiere proci recto depellere cursu ?

TIRESIAS.

Venit enim magnum donandi parca juventus,
Nec tantùm Veneris, quantùm studiosa culinæ.
Sic tibi Penelope frugi est : quæ si semel uno
De sene gustarit, tecum partita lucellum,

Does the dull rogue conceive himself a Poet
And scribble verses, that the world may know it?
In raptures cry---"The sentiments how fine!
" The verse how full! mellifluous! divine!"   130
Does he by fits with amorous passion burn?
Be sure *Penelope* supplies this turn:
Own your Penelope herself confess'd,
When last she saw, she lik'd his person best.

ULYSSES.

What, Sir? my wife, so prudent and so chaste,   135
Who never one of all the terms embrac'd,
Her suitors offer'd; can you think that she
To such vile prostitution wou'd agree?

TIRESIAS.

Your wife, good Sir! with all her innocence
Her love for you, her virtue and good sense,   140
Perhaps at last was never fairly tempted,
Her suitors came too poor, with pockets emptied;
Warm'd by the kitchen, more than Cupid's fire,
To eat and drink, their principal desire.
Shou'd a rich suitor come, that scent she'll keep;   145
As dogs once blooded, still will worry sheep:

Ut canis, â corio nunquam absterrebitur uncto.

Me sene, quod dicam, factum est.   Anus improba Thebis
Ex testamento sic est elata: cadaver
Unctum oleo largo nudis humeris tulit heres :
Scilicet elabi si posset mortua ; credo
Quòd nimiùm institerat viventi. ....

........Cautus adito :
Neu desis operæ, neve immoderatus abundes.
Difficilem et morosum offendes garrulus ; ultro
Non etiam sileas.   Davus sis comicus, atque
Stes capite obstipo, multùm similis metuenti.

Yes, trust me Sir! your ever virtuous wife,
Wou'd *share with you* the prize, and *stick to him* for life.

'Tis years ago, but well remembered still,
A sly old woman left this codicil :   150
My Heir shall bear me to my funeral pile
Naked and greas'd from top to toe with oil.
'Twas thought, indeed 'twas generally said,
Her meaning was, to give the slip when dead.
The heir, it seems, had driven things too fast,   155
And the old lady smok'd his aim at last.
Do you the moral of this tale apply,
Lest too much pains awaken jealousy.

To move as you wou'd wish and warm the heart,
Keep up, but never over act your part.   160
The cross and difficult old man will hate
The gay companion of incessant prate;
Nor in reverse of talking, wou'd he have
One that is always silent, always grave :
To please a mind in this inconstant way,   165
Take for a model---*Davus* in the play :

Obsequio grassare : mone, si increbuit aura,
Cautus uti velet carum caput : extrahe turbâ
Oppositis humeris : aurem substringe loquaci.
Importunus amat laudari ? donec, ohe jam !
Ad cælum manibus sublatis dixerit, urge, et
Crescentem tumidis infla sermonibus utrem.

Quum te servitio longo curâque levarit ;
Et certum vigilans, Quartæ esto partis Ulysses
Audieris heres : *Ergo nunc Dama sodalis*
Nusquam est ? Unde mihi tam fortem tamque fidelem ?
Sparge subinde : et, si paulùm potes, illachrymare.   Est
Gaudia prodentem vultum celare. ....

In bending posture of respect and fear,
Watch when 'tis time to speak, and when to hear.

Creep into favor by such means as these,---
If walking, there should spring an eastern breeze,   170
" My dear good Sir ! of catching cold beware,
" Nor trust yourself in this inclement air."
See you a mob ? be sure to get him in,
Only to lead him tottering out again.
Has he for praise a never ceasing thirst ?   175
Inflate the swelling bladder 'till it burst.

When Death at last shall kindly lend his aid,
To close this tedious, sycophantic trade ;
And wide awake (beware of dreams) you hear
Ulysses left five hundred pounds a year ;   180
Wringing your hands exclaim, " Is *Dama* dead ?
" A better soul to heaven never fled.
" Where shall I find another of his worth ?
" Oh never, never, never upon earth."
The thing I own is difficult, but try,   185
And if you cannot, seem at least to cry ;

..........*Sepulchrum,*

Permissum arbitrio, sine sordibus extrue: funus
Egregiè factum laudet vicinia. ....

..........*Si quis*

Fortè coheredum senior malè tussiet; huic tu
Dic, ex parte tuâ, seu fundi, sive domûs sit
Emtor, gaudentem nummo te addicere. ....

..........*Sed me*

Imperiosa trahit Proserpina: vive, valeque.

Be sure, at any rate, your outward mien
Betray no symptom of the joy within.

If left to you his monument to raise,
Spare nor for decorations, nor for praise;   190
And let each tenant of the village say
" Lord! what a funeral went thro' to day."

Is any co-heir likely to drop off?
Has he an ashtma, or a church-yard cough?
Tell him, " Dear Sir; th' estate is mine, 'tis true,   195
" But 'tis an object possibly with you:
" If so, accept it; pray Sir! be not nice,
" If not accept it, name at least the price."
But then be sure, the man to whom you give
This offer, be the one least like to live.   200

More I could sing,---But, hark! the queen of hell
Forbids my stay,---Live artful and live well.

N

SAT. VII.

DAVUS.   HORATIUS.

DAVUS.

JAMDUDUM ausculto, et cupiens, tibi dicere servus
Pauca reformido. Davusne? Ita, Davus, amicum
Mancipium domino, et frugi, quod sit satis; hoc est,
Ut vitale putes. ....

HORATIUS.

........Age, libertate Decembri
(Quando ita majores voluerunt) utere; narra.

DAVUS.

Pars hominum vitiis gaudet constanter, et urget

S A T. VII.

DAVUS. HORACE.

DAVUS.

FULL long a hearer, I begin to burn,
Tho' half afraid, to chatter in my turn.
What *Davus?*---Yes, and Sir, as I conceive,
Faithful and wise, tho' not too wise to live.

HORACE.

Well, since the times will have it so, be free,   5
And say what first comes uppermost for me.

DAVUS.

Part of mankind, however much to blame,
In what they do, yet always do the same:
Others again, less steady, you will find
This day to virtue, next to vice inclin'd.   10

Propositum ; *pars multa natat, modò reƐta capessens,*
Interdum pravis obnoxia. *Sæpe notatus*
Cum tribus annellis, modò lævâ Priscus *inani,*
Vixit inequalis, clavum ut mutaret in horas :
Ædibus ex magnis subitò se conderet, unde
Mundior exiret vix libertinus honestè :
Jam mœchus Romæ, *jam mallet doƐus* Athenis
Vivere ; *Vertumnis quotquot sunt, natus iniquis.*

Scurra Volanerius, *postquam illi justa podagra*
Contudit articulos, qui pro se tolleret atque
Mitteret in phimum talos, mercede diurnâ
ConduƐum pavit : quanto conſtantior idem
In vitiis, tanto leviùs miser, ac prior ille,
Qui jam contento, jam laxo fune laborat.

Without a watch to day, young *Tippy Bob*
To morrow sports a chain from either fob;
Between his breakfast, dinner, and the *play*,
Is dress'd in red, in green, in blue, in grey;
From house superb as any in the *park*,　　　　　15
Sinks to a *cellar*, dismal, damp and dark,
Where scarce a common servant wou'd go in,
Who valued place or character a pin:
Buck of the *Town* at six,---in six hours more
At *Cambridge*, conning *Locke* and *Euclid* o'er.　　20
Sure all the planets at his Birth combin'd
To shed their changeful influence o'er his mind.

Gamble, that worthy martyr to his gout,
The dice no longer able to throw out,
Employs a fellow upon constant pay,　　　　　25
To shake the boxes for him all the day:
Constant in vice, he feels perhaps less pain
Than who repents, yet falls to play again;
Happier who still topes on, and knows no sorrow,
Than he who drunk to day, is sick to morrow.　　30

HORATIUS.

Non dices hodie, quorsum hæc tam putida tendant,
Furcifer ?

DAVUS.

Ad te, inquam.

HORATIUS.

Quo paEto, pessime ?

DAVUS.

Laudas

Fortunam ac mores antiquæ plebis ; et idem,
Si quis ad illa Deus subitò te agat, usque recuses :
Aut quia non sentis, quod clamas, reEtius esse ;
Aut quia non firmus reEtum defendis, et hæres,
Nequicquam cæno cupiens evellere plantam.

HORACE.

Ramble no more, I can no more attend,
So bring your tale and moral to an end.

DAVUS.

Your observation, Sir! I own is true,
My tale and moral then applies to you.

HORACE.

How! saucy scoundrel, this apply to me?   35

DAVUS.

Exactly Sir, exactly to a T.

Nothing so common, as to hear you praise
The good old customs of the good old days;
When *Country Squires*, and all the better sort,
Drank humming *Ale* instead of *Punch* and *Port*:   40
When all the while, if punch or port are near,
I never see you touch a drop of *Beer*:
Either you say one thing, another think,
Or like one liquor, but another drink;
Or, reason vainly striving with desire,   45
You still stick fast and flounder in the mire.

Romæ rus optas ; absentem rusticus urbem
Tollis ad astra levis. Si nusquam es fortè vocatus
Ad cœnam, laudas securum olus ; ac, velut usquam
Vinctus eas, ita te felicem ducis amasque,
Quòd nusquam tibi sit potandum. Jusserit ad se
Mæcenas serum sub lumina prima venire
Convivam ; Nemon' oleum fert ocyus ? ecquis
Audit ? cum magno blateras clamore , fugisque.
Mulvius et scurræ, tibi non referenda precati,
Discedunt. ....

........Etenim fateor me, dixerit ille,
Duci ventre levem : nasum nidore supinor :
Imbecillus, iners, si quid vis, adde, popino.
Tu quum sis quod ego, et fortassis nequior, ultro

In Town you praise the Country, but scarce down,
Before you wish yourself again in Town:
If chance our jolly Squire shou'd fail to call
And ask you up as usual to the hall,   50
" *Davus*, say what you will of company
" But home is home, my own fire-side for me."
Scarce is this wise resolve domestic heard,
Before his honor's servant, brings a card.
" Ho ! *Davus !* where the devil are you all?   55
" Not one, when wanted, ever within call ! "
Dress'd in a moment, smart from top to toe,
Off in a bluster, quick as light you go.
Two *Curates* by your own appointment come
At six, but find no master is at home;   60
Then mutter, disappointed of their treat,
Reflections which I hardly dare repeat.

Now for myself, Sir, *Davus* not denies
He loves the savoury fumes of mutton pies;
Is slow and idle, loiters as he goes,   65
And sometimes at the tavern takes his dose:

o

Insectere, velut melior, verbisque decoris
Obvolvas vitium? ....

........Quid, si me stultior ipso
Quingentis emto drachmis deprenderis? Aufer

Me vultu terrere; manum stomachumque teneto,
·Dum, quæ Crispini *docuit me janitor, edo.*

Te conjux aliena capit, meretricula Davum:

Peccat uter nostrûm cruce dignius? Acris ubi me
Natura incendit; sub clarâ nuda lacernâ
Quæcunque excepit turgentis verbera caudæ,
Clunibus aut agitavit equum lasciva supinum,

Perhaps our passions here are much the same,
Only that your's assume a higher name;
In short the *Master* has a flow of speech
To shade his faults, which *Davus* cannot reach.　　　70

What if I prove the converse to be true,
That *Horace* is the weaker of the two?
With all his wisdom, weaker will be found,
Than the vile slave he bought for twenty pound?
Nay, hold your hand, you gave me leave to day　　　75
To speak my mind, and I will have my way.
Attend, and (if I do not greatly err)
I'll prove myself the best *Philosopher*:
For such I am, and grown a reasoner shrewd,
Taught by the porter at the *Robin Hood*.　　　80

The master must his neighbour's wife command,
I take the first that meets me on the *Strand*;
Which is the deeper sinner of the two,
The very spirit of the laws will shew.
Of amorous passion when I feel the fire,　　　85
To some obscure apartment I retire;

Dimittit neque famosum, neque solicitum, ne
Ditior aut formæ melioris meiat eodem,

Tu, quum projeƈtis insignibus, annulo equestri,
Romanoque habitu, prodis ex judice Dama
Turpis, odoratum caput obscurante lacernâ,
Non es quod simulas ? metuens induceris, atque
Altercante libidinibus tremis ossa pavore.

Quid refert, uri virgis ferroque necari
Auƈtoratus eas ; an turpi clausus in arcâ,
Quo te demisit peccati conscia herilis,

My character is safe, my mind at rest,
Nor does one jealous fear disturb my breast,
That the next fool who shall her favors buy
May have a better face or purse than I.　　　　　90

　　Now for the mischiefs of *your* amorous flame,
Your nice connection with the *married* Dame.
When my Lord *Judge*'s wig, so trim and full,
You change for *Hackney Coachman*'s all of wool;
Rush in disguise and hurry through the street,　　95
Afraid of every living soul you meet;
Pray are you not exactly to a hair,
The low bred coachman now, whose wig you wear?
But we'll admit, the house you safely get
'Twixt running, fear and love, in what a heat!　　100
Suppose you're caught,---the fair one's angry Lord
Uses at will his cudgel or his sword;
Or, stretch'd like *Abelard* beneath the knife,
You sign a bond that beggars you for life.
The mildest fate of which to be afraid,　　　　　105
Is to depend upon my lady's maid;

Contractum, genibus tangas caput ? ....

.........*Estne marito*
Matronæ peccantis in ambos justa potestas ?
In corruptorem vel justior.   Illa tamen se
Non habitu, mutatve loco, peccatve supernè ;
Quum te formidet mulier, neque credat amanti.

Ibis sub furcam prudens, dominoque furenti
Committes rem omnem et vitam et cum corpore famam.
Evâsti? metues, credo, doctusque cavebis :

In linen basket foul be stuff'd, and gone
To cool,---a *hissing horse-shoe*, like *Sir John*.※

But if the husband may revenge his shame,
And justly punish the adulterous dame ;   110
Be sure, whatever fault to her is due,
The guilt and vengeance doubly falls on you :
Your's all the risque ; for she, more wise, will stay
Secure at home, nor meet you half the way ;
She bribes no servants, puts on no disguise,   115
You take the trouble, she but shares the vice.
Ev'n then her feelings are by fear repress'd,
Nor dares she trust her lover, tho' possess'd ;
Tho' bought so dearly, not one half so free,
Or unreserv'd, as my *Strand Nymph* with me.   120

Yet for such joys, the husband's wrath you brave,
And kiss the yoke,---a voluntary slave ;
Still the same course of headstrong vice pursue,
With *Juries*, *Verdicts*, and a *Jail* in view.
Of *Doctor's Commons*, I'll suppose you free,   125
In future, sure more careful you will be ;

Quæres, quando iterum paveas, iterumque perire
Possis.   O toties servus ! quæ bellua ruptis,
Quum semel effugit, reddit se prava catenis ?

Non sum mœchus, ais.   Neque ego, Hercule, fur, ubi vasa
Prætereo sapiens argentea.   Tolle periclûm,
Jam vaga prosiliet frænis natura remotis.

Tune mihi dominus, rerum imperiis hominumque
Tot tantisque minor ? quem ter vindicta quaterque
Imposita haud umquam miserâ formidine privet ?
Adde super dictis quod non leviùs valeat : nam
Sive vicarius est, qui servo paret, uti mos
Vester ait, seu conservus : tibi quid sum ego ? Nempe
Tu, mihi qui imperitas, aliis servis miser, atque
Duceris, ut nervis alienis mobile signum.

No, in a month, the self same course you run,
Of fear and danger, fond to be undone.
Will then your spaniel, free to range the plain,
Return, and court the collar and the chain ?   130
No, *Ranger* will not,---but with all his skill,
His sense and wariness, the *Master* will.

But I am no adulterer, you cry,----
No, please your honor, nor a thief am I:
But take from each the hazard of his life,   135
I steal your plate, and you your neighbour's wife.
What, you my master ! you to domineer,
The slave yourself of passion and of fear ?
Whom not a club of *Jacobins* cou'd free,
Nor *Paine* in person rouse to liberty ?   140
But to pursue this matter further still,
Call me your Servant,---Slave, Sir, if you will :
Still in another sense, we are but brothers ;
I am your slave, and you, the slave of others:
Lord over me, but, with a lord or 'squire,   145
The puppet dancing as he pulls the wire.

P

HORATIUS.

Quisnam igitur liber?

DAVUS.

   Sapiens; sibi qui imperiosus:
Quem neque pauperies, neque mors, nec vincula terrent:
Responsare cupidinibus, contemnere honores
Fortis, et in seipso totus teres atque rotundus,
Externi ne quid valeat per leve morari;
In quem manca ruit semper Fortuna. Potesne
Ex his, ut proprium, quid noscere?........

      ....Quinque talenta
Poscit te mulier, vexat, foribusque repulsum
Perfundit gelidâ: rursus vocat. Eripe turpi
Colla jugo: liber, liber sum, dic age. Non quis;
Urget enim mentem dominus non lenis, et acres
Subjectat lasso stimulos, versatque negantem.

HORACE.

Who then is free?

DAVUS.

     The wise man, he who knows
No fear of death, or any human woes :
Who fears not want, who to no lusts will yield,
Proof against wealth, against ambition steel'd ;   150
Who sees the random darts of fortune fly
And smiles secure in virtue's panoply.
Now of this picture, and 'tis fairly shewn,
Is there a feature you can call your own ?

     For twenty pounds *Belinda* asks a note,   155
" Madam I have it not,"   ' *Then pawn your coat.*'
Or pawn your coat, or stand the viler shame
Of cooling from a wash I blush to name.
Now shew yourself a man, and take affront,
No, Master *Horace*, no, depend upon't   160
Passion will get the better in the main,
And blindly carry you to *Bell* again.

Vel quum Pausiacâ torpes, insane, tabellâ,
Qui peccas minùs atque ego, quum Fulvî, Rutubæque,
Aut Placideiani contento poplite miror
Prælia, rubricâ pi&a aut carbone, velut si
Re verâ pugnent, feriant vitentque moventes
Arma viri? Nequam, et cessator Davus : at ipse
Subtilis veterum judex, et callidus audis.

Nîl ego, si ducor libo fumante ; tibi ingens
Virtus, atque animus cœnis responsat opimis.

Of pictures, I have heard, you nothing know,
Yet daily to the *Shakespear* you must go;
Lounge round the room, remark on every print,   165
" This has some merit, that has nothing in't."
Now shou'd poor *Davus* happen but to stop,
Caught by some Sign-post Painting at a shop;
Where *Humphreys* and *Mendoza* shall engage,
As big as life, and on as big a stage;   170
So like, that many a country fellow vows
He hears distinct as possible the blows;
He is, forsooth, an idle, loitering dog,
Down comes the whip, and all prepar'd to flog;
But *you*, Sir *!* tho' a loiterer just the same,   175
Have got a nice discerning critic's name !

If where the savoury sausage scents the street,
The good for nothing rascal stops to eat,
Davus commits a terrible offence;
But you, Sir! are the pink of abstinence;   180
A man of such stern virtue, that, I know,
Ask'd to the costliest feast, you'd answer, No.

Obsequium ventris mihi perniciosius est cur ?
Tergo plector enim : qui tu impunitior illa,
Quæ parvo sumu nequeunt, obsonia captas ?
Nempe inamarescunt epulæ sine fine petitæ,
Illusique pedes vitiosum ferre recusant
Corpus. ....

........An hic peccat, sub noctem qui puer uvam
Furtivâ mutat strigili ? qui prædia vendit,
Nil servile, gulæ parens, habet ? Adde, quòd idem
Non horam tecum esse potes, non otia rectè
Ponere ; teque ipsum vitas fugitivus et erro ;
Jam vino quærens, jam somno fallere curam :
Frustra : nam comes atra premit, sequiturque fugacem.

If I enjoy good eating, must it be,
No crime in you, a deadly sin in me?
In this, alas! the sad distinction lies,   185
My back must suffer for my belly's vice;
But shall *your* banquet 'scape the vengeance due,
Because no master shakes a cane at you?
No! soon your wines shall nauseate on the taste,
And the pall'd stomach loath the frequent feast;   190
Soon shall your trembling limbs their aid deny
To bear the frame worn down with gluttony.

Your stable boy shall steal a curry-comb,
And change it for an apple or a plumb;
Now will you think the man no greater sinner,   195
Who gives a fortune for a single dinner?
Added to this, you cannot be alone,
And if you are, so cursed peevish grown,
That I am glad, the house in peace to keep,
To see you downright drunk, or sound asleep;   200
For so it is, reflections of some kind,
Half drunk or *half* asleep, disturb your mind.

HORATIUS.

Unde mihi lapidem?

DAVUS.

Quorsum est opus?

HORATIUS.

Unde sagittas?

DAVUS.

Aut insanit homo, aut versus facit.

HORATIUS.

Ocius hinc te
Ni rapis, accedes opera agro nona Sabino.

HORACE.

A stone, does no one hear me? bring a stone,----

DAVUS.

Be moderate, Sir! in truth there's need of none.

HORACE.

Oh! that my loaded pistol now I had!   205

DAVUS.

The man is turning Poet, or stark mad.

HORACE.

Out of my sight this moment, saucy knave,
Or to *Barbadoes* back, for life a Slave.

-

Q

SAT. VIII.

HORATIUS.   FUNDANIUS.

HORATIUS.

*U*T Nasidieni *juvit te cœna beati?*
Nam mihi convivam quærenti, dictus heri illuc
De medio potare die. ....

FUNDANIUS.

........*Sic, ut mihi nunquam*
In vitâ fuerit meliùs. ....

HORATIUS.

........*Dic (si grave non est)*
Quæ prima iratum ventrem placaverit esca.

S A T. VIII.

HORACE.   FUNDANIUS.

HORACE.

WELL, Sir! what kind of evening with the *Mayor?*
For, to my disappointment, you were there;
When yesterday, in all my life before
I never wanted a companion more:
By various gossips I have understood,   5
You drank as long as drinking cou'd be good.

FUNDANIUS.

A day so pleasant, that upon my soul,
I never spent a better on the whole.

HORACE.

Indeed! then pray particulars repeat,
And give me every *Item* of the treat.   10

FUNDANIUS.

In primis Lucanus aper ; leni fuit Austro
Captus, ut aiebat cœnæ pater ; acria circùm
Rapula, lactucæ, radices, qualia lassum
Pervellunt stomachum, siser, alec, fæcula Coa.

His ubi sublatis, puer altè cinctus acernam
Gausape purpureo mensam pertersit, et alter
Sublegit quodcunque jaceret inutile, quodque
Posset cœnantes offendere : ut Attica virgo
Cum sacris Cereris, procedit fuscus Hydaspes
Cæcuba vina ferens ; Alcon, Chium maris expers.
Hic herus : Albanum, Mæcenas, sive Falernum
Te magis appositis delectat ; habemus utrumque :
Divitias miseras ! ....

FUNDANIUS.

For course the first, two haunches were assign'd,
Kill'd in the forest, in a *southern* wind;
So said our host, and so I shou'd suppose,
If I might form my judgment by my nose:
A dish to whet the appetite stood by   15
With *Lettuce, Radishes* and *Celery*:
On either side were various sauces seen,
As *Katchup, Soy, Anchovies* and the *Quin.*

    This course remov'd, a footman in a trice
Spread a clean cloth of damask white and nice;   20
And true it is, however like a joke,
The cloths were damask, but the table oak:
The scatter'd fragments, next he clear'd away,
For neatness sake,---or for another day.
Then next advanc'd, in solemn pace and slow,   25
As in procession at the *City Shew,*
Pompey the black, and *John* with different wine,
This from the *Cape,* the other from the *Rhine,*
Tho' neither knew the Sea, or ever cross'd the *Line.*

........*Sed queis cœnantibus unà,*
Fundani, *pulchrè fuerit tibi, nosse laboro.*

FUNDANIUS.

Summus ego, et prope me Viscus Thurinus, *et infra*
(Si memini) Varius ; *cum* Servilio Balatrone
Vibidius, *quos* Mæcenas *adduxerat umbras :*
Nomentanus *erat supra ipsum :* Porcius *infra,*
Ridiculus totas semel absorbere placentas.
Nomentanus ad hoc, qui, si quid fortè lateret,

Instant our host,---" *Mæcenas*, that is *Hock*;   30
" And, if you like it, never fear my stock:
" Choice in my wines, I keep of every sort,
" But all poor stuff, I think, compar'd with *Port*.

HORACE.

Now, dear *Fundanius*, tell me if you can,
Who were your jovial party to a man.   35

FUNDANIUS.

* *Mæcenas* then was at the upper end,
And next to him on either side a friend:
For he, to grace the party, carried two;
Vibidius, and *Servilius Balatro*.
The next to them, as not in rank so high,   40
Were plac'd *Thurinus*, *Varius*, and I.
Our landlord at the bottom took his seat
Between two friends, to carve or praise the meat;
Portius was there, his humour in the main,
To swallow cheese-cakes till he choak'd again.   45
On t'other side, the Mayor's supreme delight,
Sat *Nomentanus*, a true parasite;
Officious as his patron's heart cou'd wish,
To call attention to each different dish:

Indice monstraret digito. Nam cætera turba
Nos, inquam, cœnamus aves, conchylia, pisces,
Longè dissimilem noto celantia succum :
Ut vel continuò patuit, quum passeris assi, et
Ingustata mihi porrexerit ilia Rhombi.

Post hoc me docuit melimela rubere, minorem
Ad lunam delecta. Quid hoc intersit, ab ipso
Audieris meliùs. Tum Vibidius Balatroni :
Nos, nisi damnosè bibimus, moriemur inulti ;
Et calices poscit majores. ....

For we, who like true *Common Council Men,*   50
Stick to the rule of cut and come again,
By his account, devour'd with hungry haste,
Fish, flesh and fowl, regardless of their taste;
Things so disguis'd, he said, so richly done,
For what they were, they never cou'd be known.   55
To prove his words, and all my doubts confound,
He help'd me to a *Flounder* and *Cod's sound;*
And sure enough, he safely might have swore,
I never tasted such a dish before.

   Our Landlord now had enter'd a dispute,   60
About the proper time to gather fruit;
The time he said, tho' mostly thought too soon,
Was just beyond the middle of the moon:
Quite scientific this,---but I must leave
The reasons of his rule, for him to give.   65
'Twas now *Mæcenas'* friends began to smoke
Their stupid treat, and turn it to a joke.
One to the other whispers low and sly,
" Come let's be even with, and drink him dry:"

........*Vertere pallor*
Tum parochi faciem, nil sic metuentis ut acres
Potores : vel quòd maledicunt liberiùs ; vel
Fervida quòd subtile exsurdant vina palatum.
Invertunt Aliſanis vinaria tota
Vibidius Balatroque, secutis omnibus : imi
Convivæ lecti nihilum nocuere lagenis.

Adfertur squillas inter muræna natantes
In patinâ porrecta.   Sub·hoc herus : Hæc gravida, inquit,

Then bids the servant larger glasses bring;   70
" Sir, with your leave, a bumper to the King."

His *Worship*, at the very word turn'd pale
And look'd as sour, nay sourer than his ale:
Nothing, it seems, he dreads so much on earth,
As guests too fond of Bacchanalian mirth;   75
Since drinking oft provokes censorious jest
And blunts the nice distinction of the taste.
The humour took, and quick as it cou'd pass,
Each gave his toast, and swallow'd down his glass:
The guests below, too much within controul,   80
Were mark'd to be the soberest of the whole.

Now came a Turbot, swimming in a dish,
Garnish'd with shrimps, the nicest of shell-fish.
Our host again,---" *Mæcenas*, this was caught
" In spawn, for after, 'tis not worth a groat;   85
" And, Sir! my sauces, you will own, surpass
" The best of *Farley*'s or of Mrs. *Glasse*:
" This gravy for the fish, so rich and high,
" Is oil,---the best that *Florence* can supply,

Capta est ; deterior post partum carne futura.
His mistum jus est oleo, quod prima Venafri
.Pressit cella ; garo de succis piscis Iberi :
Vino quinquenni, verùm citra mare nato,
Dum coquitur : coĉto Chium sic convenit, ut non
Hoc magis ullum aliud ; pipere albo, non sine aceto,
Quod Methymneam vitio mutaverit uvam.
Erucas virides, inulas ego primus amaras
Monstravi incoquere : illotos Curtillus echinos,
Ut meliùs muriâ, quam testa marina remittit.

" Anchovies genuine,---for, to have them so,   90
" I fetch them from the *Archipelago* ;
" *Madeira*---five year's old, that twice has cross'd
" The *Line* ; white Pepper from *Sumatra*'s coast ;
" My Vinegar,---nor common is, nor plain,
" But twice distill'd and made from best *Champaign* ;   95
" These at the first,---and, when it well has boil'd,
" Old *Mountain*---if before, your sauce is spoil'd.
" To say the truth, I never trust to book
" In these affairs, or even to my cook ;
" But always see myself the proper brine,   100
" The proper oil and quantity of wine.
" 'Twas I that first preserv'd the *Kidney Bean*,
" And kept it thro' the winter, fresh and green ;
" I first the meadow mushroom treasur'd up,
" To mix in precious powder with my soup ;   105
" I best of any one, my *Oysters* fat,
" But *B-mb-r G-sc-gne* beats me at a *Sprat.*"

But now the mournful muse I must invoke,
To sing events too serious for a joke.

Interea suspensa graves aulæa ruinas
In patinam fecere, trahentia pulveris atri
Quantum non Aquilo Campanis excitat agris.

Nos majus veriti, postquam nihil esse pericli
Sensimus, erigimur. Rufus *posito capite, ut si*
Filius immaturus obisset, flere. Quis esset
Finis, ni sapiens sic Nomentanus *amicum*
Tolleret ? Heu ! Fortuna, quis est crudelior in nos
Te Deus ? ut semper gaudes illudere rebus
Humanis ! Varius *mappâ compescere risum*
Vix poterat. Balatro, *suspendens omnia naso,*

High over all, suspended by a tye   110
Too loose, there hung an ancient canopy;
Where safe and undisturb'd full many a day,
Spiders by dozens in their cobwebs lay:
Down came the dusty weight; and, in the fall,
Smother'd the table, company and all.   115
Not such a dust in August fills our eyes,
From new-rais'd Cavalry at exercise.

After some minutes taken to recover,
And satisfy ourselves the worst was over,
Our host upon his hand reclin'd his head,   120
And wept, as if his only son were dead;
'Till *Nomentanus* nobly strove to raise
His spirits, by reflexions such as these.
" Oh ! envious fortune ! what a piteous spite !
" In human crosses thus to take delight !"   125
Varius polite, and fearful to offend,
With laughing, stopp'd the fit with napkin's end.
The humorous *Balatro* resolv'd, at least,
To make it but a tragi-comic feast;

Hæc est conditio vivendi, aiebat; eoque
Responsura tuo nunquam est par fama labori.
Tene, ut ego accipiar lautè, torquerier omni
Solicitudine distriĉtum? ne panis adustus,
Ne malè conditum jus apponatur; ut omnes
Præcinĉti reĉtè pueri comtique ministrent?
Adde hos præterea casus; aulæa ruant si,
Ut modò; si patinam pede lapsus frangat agaso.

Sed convivatoris, uti ducis, ingenium res
Adversæ nudare solent, celare secundæ
Nasidienus ad hæc: Tibi Dî, quæcunque preceris,
Commoda dent; ita vir bonus es, convivaque comis;
Et socias poscit. Tum u leĉto quoque videres
Stridere secretâ divisos aure susurros.

And thus with decent gravity began,   130
" Ah Sir ! the fate, the cruel fate of man !
" How common, all his time and pains to spend
" In search of fame, and lose it in the end !
" Thus you, who neither cost nor trouble spare
" To entertain us with the best of fare,   135
" Your servants dress in liveries so gay,
" To crown the neatness of the festive day,
" Must still be subject to a curtain's fall,
" To marr your pains at once, and ruin all."

" *Landlords* and *Generals* I oft have thought   140
" May to a fair comparison be brought ;
" This against adverse battles must bear up,
" That must not mind a broken dish or cup :
" Each, when he bears the sudden strokes of fate
" With even fortitude, alike is great."   145
Our *Mayor*, with rapture sparkling in his eyes,
" Oh, best of friends ! oh, sweetest fellow ! " cries ;
Then leaves the table with apparent ease,
And us to laugh and comment as we please.

Nullos his mallem ludos spectasse. ....

HORATIUS.
........*Sed illa*
Redde, age, quæ deinceps risisti. ....

FUNDANIUS.
........Vibidius *dum*
Quærit de pueris, num sit quoque fracta lagena,
Quòd sibi poscenti non dentur pocula ; dumque
Ridetur fictis rerum, Balatrone *secundo ;*
Nasidiene, redis mutatæ frontis, ut arte
Emendaturus fortunam. ....

........*Deinde secuti*
Mazonomo pueri magno discerpta ferentes
Membra gruis sparsi sale multo, non sine farre,
Pinguibus et ficis pastum jecur anseris albi,

In short, dear *Horace,* as I said before,   150
No comedy cou'd ever please me more.

HORACE.

Still my impertinence excuse, my friend,
And let me have your story to the end.

FUNDANIUS.

Vibidius then, half earnest and half joke,
Call'd to the boys,---" Are all the bottles broke ?"   155
But just as *Balatro* had crack'd his jest,
In came again the founder of the feast;
Resolv'd, as did his countenance proclaim,
To match, if possible, the slippery dame.

Of footmen, cooks and scullions, the whole herd,   160
Now follow at his heels with course the third :
In a huge dish, the first a *Turkey* bore,
Ready cut up, and froth'd with salt and flour;
Next came a *Goose,* on milk and white bread fed;
Then *wings* of *Hares,* the tenderest parts, he said,   165
Far better than the *back;* to crown the whole
Woodcocks, whose *legs* were roasted to a coal;

Et leporum avulsos, ut multò suaviùs, armos,
Quàm si cum lumbis quis edit. Tum pectore adusto
Vidimus et merulas poni, et sine clune palumbes;
Suaves res, si non causas narraret earum et
Naturas dominus: quem nos sic fugimus ulti,
Ut nihil omnino gustaremus, velut illis
Canidia afflâsset, pejor serpentibus Afris.

And, as the last perfection of his art,
Broil'd *Pidgeons,* but without the *hinder part.*
Delicious fare !---but still he kept his prate   170
About the qualities of this and that,
'Till, out of humour, not a soul wou'd stay,
But took his hat, and grumbling went away ;
Sick, as if suffer'd in his pans to look,
Or see the dirty fingers of his cook.   175

N O T E S.

~~~~~~~~~

HAVING premised in my Preface that I am no *Critic*, I must beg to observe to the *Classical Reader*, that, if in any of the following Notes I should seem to him to assume that Character, I do not give or mean to give my opinion as of any Authority.

* *Jove once thought fit*] This passage is very pleasingly paraphrased in a paper of the *Spectator*; where the offer is supposed to have been actually made, accepted, and repented of. I confess I have amplified here, as in other places, only because I could not keep up to the conciseness of my Author and be clear myself.

* *As oft the Boy*] I am aware that *Horace* carries his allusion back much nearer to Infancy and the Alphabet than I have done. But in modern Practice, the idea of encouraging Boys to get their Lessons by Nuts, Gingerbread, and the like, gives an idea of the mere *Dame's* School; which I think is going too far. I have often known a humorous story from the Master arising out of it, put a whole class in humour with a dry and difficult lesson, which otherwise would have been lost upon them, both for instruction and amusement. Upon this recollection, I have taken the liberty to vary here from the immediate sense of the passage.

* *Like for example's sake*] The Edition by Mr. *Francis* is the only one I have seen that begins the Dialogue here; and I follow it for this reason: it appears to me that our Poet purposely throws an opportunity in the *Miser's* way of justifying his love and pursuit of money, upon the same principles that Men in *general* act, viz. *Ut in otia tuta recedant*: and then puts the natural simile of the Ant into his mouth, only to turn it against him, with the pleasant severity that follows.—This Trap set for him, I own strikes me, as a peculiar beauty in the Satire.

* *Dancer possess'd*] This unaccountable Being died in the year 1794, immensely rich, both in land and money. It is recorded of him, amongst other miserable devices to get money, that he would personate the distressed beggar, and in that character thankfully receive the most trifling donations that were offered him. He died indeed a *natural* death; and I am inclined to think, notwithstanding the pains taken by commentators to ascertain the genealogy of his Assassin, that the original *Ummidius* or *Humidius* (if not a fictitious name) might make the same quiet exit; and that our Poet in the spirit of his Satire, only assigned him the death such a wretch might seem to deserve.

* *But to the point again*] Our Poet at the commencement of this Satire, treats of the discontentedness of mankind in *general*; he then breaks off and addresses himself to the *Miser* only. I have taken the liberty of imagining, that by *Illuc, unde abii, redeo*, he means to return to his first general

proposition, and that the following lines no longer apply to the *Miser* in particular. I know that strict grammatical construction does not favor this liberty; but it appears to me to give more spirit and variety to the Satire, than if we restrict it to the same individual.

* *Where to the gentle*] I have purposely omitted the cruel piece of Satire that follows on *Balbinus :* Surely the ridiculous passion here attributed to him can hardly be conceived to exist. At any rate I must think that defects in our friends at all equal to this in personal beauty, if they do not disgust, neither can nor ought to delight us.

* *'Tis thus, tho'* Siddons] Zeno the founder of the *Stoic* Sect advanced of wisdom (which implied the subjection of the passions to our reason) that it made a man *every thing*. This bold and *figurative* expression was taken up by some of his followers, of perplexed understandings, in a *literal* sense, and led to the absurd inexplicable paradoxes our Poet here and in various other places so pleasantly ridicules.

* *Like Dr.* Johnson *to a* Scot] Whoever wishes to see an instance of this rough language has only to read Mr. *Boswell's* account of his own introduction to him, and other anecdotes of the Doctor in print.

* *A heat that splits the pavement*--------Anon.
Or great Dubartas] Mr. *Dryden*, in his Preface to the *Spanish Friar*, says of these lines, that, when a young man, he used to admire them as the most perfect model of the *Sublime in Poetry* he had any conception of.

* ------*A hissing horse-shoe like Sir John*] This passage might lead us to conclude that *Shakspeare* had a better knowledge of the ancients, than the Author of an ingenious *treatise on his learning* is inclined to allow him; but perhaps falsely : For that two lively imaginations at work upon the same subject, should hit upon the same thoughts and even expressions, is not very improbable. As Mr. *Francis* remarks, "Next to be compassed like a good Bilboe in the circumference of a peck; hilt "to point; heel to head;" seems almost a literal translation of *Horace*. The comparison of the *Knight* upon his immersion to a *hissing horse-shoe*, is peculiarly our English Poet's.

* *Mæcenas then*] As I have endeavoured to adapt this Satire to modern manners, I have not preserved the places of the company, as in the original, since it could not be reconciled with modern customs; and because all the purpose seems to be as well answered by placing *Mæcenas, Fundanius,* &c. at the top, and the *Mayor* with his parasites at the bottom. If any one wishes to have their exact situation, he may find an accurate representation of it in the edition by Mr. *Francis*.

www.ingramcontent.com/pod-product-compliance
Lightning Source LLC
Chambersburg PA
CBHW021125020726
47500CB00003B/928